CW00664906

How Steeple Sinderby Wand

J. L. Carr was born in 1912 and attended the village school at Carlton Miniott, North Yorkshire, and Castleford Grammar School. For many years a head teacher at a primary school in Kettering, he left teaching in 1967 to set up a small publishing imprint called the Quince Tree Press which published standard poets in a series of 'Pocket Books', idiosyncratic historical county maps and unlikely dictionaries in order to support the writing of further fiction.

He published eight novels altogether: *A Day in Summer* (1964); *A Season in Sinji* (1967); *The Harpole Report* (1972); *How Steeple Sinderby Wanderers Won the FA Cup* (1975); *A Month in the Country* (1980), which won the Guardian Fiction Prize and was shortlisted for the Booker Prize; *The Battle of Pollocks Crossing* (1985), which was also shortlisted for the Booker Prize; *What Hetty Did* (1988) and *Harpole & Foxberrow General Publishers* (1992).

J. L. Carr died in Northamptonshire in 1994 but the Quince Tree Press continues to be run as a back-bedroom business by his family and has kept all the novels available in his own editions.

D. J. Taylor was born in 1960. He is the author of eleven novels, including *English Settlement* (1996), which won a Grinzane Cavour prize; *Derby Day* (2011), longlisted for the Man Booker Prize; and *The Windsor Faction* (2013). His non-fiction includes *Thackeray* (1999) and *Orwell: The Life*, which won the 2003 Whitbread Prize for Biography. He lives on Norwich with his wife, the novelist Rachel Hore, and their three children.

J. L. CARR

*How Steeple Sinderby
Wanderers Won the FA Cup*

With an Introduction by D. J. Taylor

PENGUIN BOOKS

PENGUIN CLASSICS

UK | USA | Canada | Ireland | Australia
India | New Zealand | South Africa

Penguin Books is part of the Penguin Random House group of companies
whose addresses can be found at global.penguinrandomhouse.com.

First published in 1975
First published in Penguin Classics 2016
004

Copyright © Bob Carr, 1975
Introduction copyright © D. J. Taylor, 2016

The moral rights of the author and introducer have been asserted

Set in 11.25/14 pt Dante MT Std
Typeset by Jouve (UK), Milton Keynes
Printed in Great Britain by Clays Ltd, St Ives plc

A CIP catalogue record for this book is available from the British Library

ISBN: 978-0-241-25234-5

www.greenpenguin.co.uk

MIX
Paper from
responsible sources
FSC® C018179

Penguin Random House is committed to a
sustainable future for our business, our readers
and our planet. This book is made from Forest
Stewardship Council® certified paper.

Introduction

> Mr Slingsby (Capt.), reporting on *Interim Progress*, stated that
> his team had defeated Hackthorn Young Conservatives (away)
> 13–0, N. Baddesley Congs Tennis & Football Club (home)
> 14–0, Bennington British Rail (away) 12–0 and Aston Villa (at
> Wolverhampton) 2–1. The Chairman commented favourably
> on these statistics . . .

J. L. Carr – his baptismal names were Joseph Lloyd, but friends
knew him as Jim – died in February 1994 at the age of eighty-
one. The obituaries were long and appreciative, without ever
quite getting beyond the bank of fortifications that the deceased
had erected before his highly enigmatic personality and the
faint air of concealment that hung over nearly every aspect of
his life. This, after all, was a man who, when asked to supply
jacket copy for an American edition of one of his novels, vouchsafed the single sentence 'J. L. Carr lives in England', who left
bits of fake medieval statuary lying around rural churchyards
'to give people something to think about' and whose funeral
was enlivened by the last-minute appearance of a beautiful
black-clad young woman in high heels whom the other mourn-
ers strained to identify. According to his biographer Byron
Rogers, who lurked amid the horde of journalists, readers, ex-
pupils and the ornaments of advisory committees on church
architecture, such had been the rigid compartmentalization of

Carr's eight decades on the planet that nearly all those present had come to bid farewell to different men.

The bare outline of Carr's progress through mid-twentieth-century England offers scarcely a hint of the vat of idiosyncrasy that boiled away within him. In strict biographical terms, he was the son of a stationmaster-cum-Methodist lay reader from North Yorkshire who, heading south to pursue a career in schoolteaching, ended up as the headmaster of a primary school in Kettering, Northamptonshire. Here he was remembered as a pioneer of what would now be known as 'child-centred education' but to Carr seemed ordinary common sense: the school gates were left unlocked so that pupils could play in the grounds at night; a history trip to the water meadows at Wellingborough involved the dispatch of an Armada of message-filled bottles and a complaint from the clerk of the Nene River Board, while the all-inclusive sports days incorporated Arithmetic Races, with blackboards set up for competitors to complete sums as they made their way around the course. Then, as Carr moved into his fifties, there came a change of direction. Having spent time at a Workers' Educational Association creative writing class and published a well-received first novel (*A Day in Summer*, 1963), he gave up Highfields Primary and, with the loyal support of his wife, Sally, capital of £1,600 and a back bedroom pressed into service as office space, set up as the tiniest of small publishers.

The Carrs began by issuing sixpenny booklet selections of the classics, hand-drawn maps of the English counties and one or two bona fide originals, such as *Carr's Dictionary of English Queens, Kings' Wives, Celebrated Paramours, Handfast Spouses and Royal Changelings*, which, as experts pointed out, would have sold even better had the more technically accurate 'concubines' replaced 'handfast spouses'. Carr, who as he put it venerated his father's memory, was inflexible on this point. Meanwhile, in the intervals between repping his wares around remote parts of the British Isles and shaking his head over the bundles of letters sent in by children with suspiciously mature hand-writing keen to take advantage of their twopenny discount, he continued to labour at what, it is fair to say, he regarded as the really serious business of his life. There were another seven novels, written at four- or five-year intervals, with wildly dif-fering levels of success. In the cash-strapped mid-1970s some remaindered copies of *The Harpole Report* (1972) were supposed to have paid a butcher's bill, but both *A Month in the Country* (1980), later filmed with Kenneth Branagh and Colin Firth, and *The Battle of Pollocks Crossing* (1985) made the Booker shortlist. It was entirely typical of Carr that, having achieved this feat, he should have given London publishing up for good and resolved to bring out his last two books (*What Hetty Did*, 1988, and *Harpole and Foxberrow General Publishers*, 1992) himself.

Like nearly everything he wrote, *How Steeple Sinderby Wanderers Won the FA Cup*, his fourth novel, first published in 1975 by Alan Ross's London Magazine Editions, is a mixture of the prosaically down-to-earth and the unutterably fantastic. On the one hand, its grounding in the realities of amateur football, where the teams change into their kit in an old LNER railway carriage and the reek of embrocation steals along the touch-line like river fog, is horribly authentic: reissuing the book himself shortly before he died, Carr larkily included a photo-graph of a real-life football team, which turns out to be a North Yorkshire XI from the early 1930s, with the author himself perched on one knee at the end of the front row. On the other, its premise comes straight from a post-war boys' comic like the *Victor* or the *Eagle* – nothing less than a straightforward exer-cise in wish-fulfilment, in which a village side, trained up by Dr Kossuth, an émigré Hungarian academic who has applied his deductive intelligence to the first principles of sport, and supported by the tyrannical local magnate, Mr Fangfoss, sees off several First Division teams in a triumphal cavalcade that runs all the way to Wembley Stadium.

The vehicle for this fantasia on the state of our national game *circa* 1973 – a time-frame confirmed by the references to Alan Hardaker, Football League secretary until 1979 – is, by and large, pastiche. This much can be inferred from the breathless match commentaries of the local newshound, seventeen-year-old Alice 'Ginchy' Trigger ('Her heroes were Thomas Hardy and Monty Python'), the epic parody of Neville Cardus-style broadsheet sports reporting courtesy of *The Times*'s 'Nigel Kelmscott-Jones' ('you never would have guessed that both his prep and public schools played rugger, or that he loathed all games and was just filling in with sport until his uncle could find an excuse to winkle out the Paris correspondent . . .') and the *Sun*'s reaction to the news that this previously unheard-of hamlet had drawn Hartlepool in the first round proper ('Old Grandfer Fangfoss, trainer of the villagers, squeezed a chuckle from his toothless jaws as he sat over a noggin beside his cottage door. "Oi sez our lads'll win 'em, mi jolleys," he piped, running a horny hand over his luscious sixteen year old bride's bouncy boobies.')

If all this sometimes threatens to get dangerously out of hand, then there are always one or two uncomfortable truths lurking at the story's edge with the capacity to undermine the basic high-spiritedness of its attack. Carr's *forte* as a writer, it might be said, is the faint air of wistfulness that always attends even his most comic scenes, the barely disguised feeling that despite the best efforts of its cast life will never turn out quite how they want it to, that disappointment lies just around the corner and that happiness needs to be grasped at in the split second before it turns into stark disillusion. And so Steeple Sinderby ('popn 547, height above sea-level in the Dry Season,

32 feet'), as well as harbouring any amount of neighbourliness and good-fellowship, is also a Gehenna of drift and frustration. Joe Gidner, its punctilious chronicler, is an absolutely typical Carr specimen, a bruised and purposeless twenty-something who, having 'had this trouble and left theological college', answers a newspaper ad and finds himself living in the village schoolmaster's house, where he combines the writing of greet-ings-cards verses with looking after his host's invalid wife. Desperate for something to give meaning to his life, Joe finds it in the secretaryship of the football club, here in its moment of triumph, only for the dream to puncture as soon as it has taken shape. 'I know what you're looking for,' Mr Fangfoss tells him at the novel's close, when the two men bump into each other on a January afternoon six months after the final. 'But it's gone, and it'll never come back.'

A Month in the Country's finale strikes exactly the same note, with its bleak assurance that past life can never be properly recaptured and all we can do is treasure the memories gath-ered up along the way. At the same time, *How Steeple Sinderby Wanderers Won the FA Cup* is something more than a comedy in which, mysteriously, no one is ever happy and no character can rest until his, or her, illusions about existence have been ruth-lessly dispelled. It is also, obliquely and with maximum stealth, a state of the nation novel, or rather a novel about an alterna-tive nation that subsists, in conditions of relative neglect, on the first one's border. 'People don't know about rural England between the last Mystery Autumn Foliage Coach Trip and the Mystery Blossom Journey into Spring,' Gidner reflects at one point. 'Mud, fog, dripping trees, blackness, floods, mighty rushing winds under doors that don't fit, damp hassocks, stick-ing organ keys, stone floors and that dreadful smell of decay.' Like his friend Penelope Fitzgerald's *The Bookshop* (1978), this is a bulletin from the English margins, where the prescriptions of

Westminster and Fleet Street count for very little and the media racket reduces itself to the faintest perceptible hum.

It is not simply that Carr devotes several pages to the history of his imaginary fenland village, its spoof entry in Pevsner's *Buildings of England*, its 'peasant poet' Thomas Dadds, on whose grave the local children strew flowers on the anniversary of his birth, and whose mournful verse Gidner is given to quoting. Much more telling, perhaps, is the way in which Steeple Sinderby is used as a stick with which to beat the tinsel-town values of the media scrum that descends once the team has seen off Leeds United in the Fourth Round. Mr Fangfoss, in particular, is seized upon by the newspapers, has his pronouncements on such topics as the Common Market and the nationalized industries reproduced in a best-selling paperback entitled *Chairman Fangfoss's Words* ('there had never been such a man for voicing popular prejudice since Enoch Powell retired,' Carr helpfully glosses) and at one stage grants a live television interview to a BBC personality in which he loses his temper, offers some choice remarks about the work-shy, denounces medium and messenger alike, and demands to be switched off forthwith. The subsequent mail delivery amounts to eleven sacks.

A polygamous local farmer who assumes the chairmanship of the football club merely because he is in charge of everything else, Mr Fangfoss exemplifies Carr's attitude to the wider landscapes beyond the Sinderby window. Half of him clearly regards the man whose Rural District Council election address consists of the eight words 'If elected I will keep down the rates' as a kind of monstrous ogre complacently ruling the roost over people who would be better off without him, but the other half rather sympathizes with his idea that the modern world is essentially a swindle in which good nature is stifled and trampled upon by catchpenny moralists and obfuscating

Whitehall bureaucrats, and the only way of ameliorating the human lot is simply to let ordinary people get on with their lives, free from the interference of the state. The explanation for this larger-than-life quality lies in the fact that he appeals to Carr's mischievous side, which is always keen on seeing just how far his characters can go, sometimes seeming to rebuke them for their folly while quietly cheering their good sense and at all times hanging an atmospheric smokescreen over the book which extends even as far as its location.

Where, when it comes down to it, *is* Steeple Sinderby? This is apparently a fenland village – the main crop is sugar beet – but the solitary professional fixture which Dr Kossuth attends in his attempt to comprehend the principles of football takes place at Leicester City's Filbert Street ground. The names of the towns nearby and some of the characters are taken from locales as various as North Yorkshire (Slingsby, Hackthorn), the East Riding (Fangfoss) and Radnorshire (Cascob). The air of mystery which hangs over Steeple Sinderby's exact location – possibly the westernmost edge of Cambridgeshire or a few miles over the south Lincolnshire border – extends to the team's progress in the cup, where the first round is for some reason followed by the fourth, and there are apparently only two more games between that and the final, itself played against Glasgow Rangers owing to a rule change which for the first time admits Scottish clubs into the competition.

The reader who comes fresh to Carr's work might reasonably assume that this is the result of simple negligence. Long-term fans would probably counter that, on the contrary, he knew exactly what he was doing and that the novel's procedural inconsistencies are quite deliberate, the natural consequence of a writer who is, above all things, determined not to give himself away, to keep some part of his considerable technical weaponry in reserve. Carr was modest about his achievements: shortly after *A Month in the Country*'s appearance on the wide screen he declared that all he had really tried to do was to create a few characters and speed them around the page in a plausible way. But *How Steeple Sinderby Wanderers Won the FA Cup* is an extraordinary performance, simultaneously one of the greatest football novels ever written and a penetrating report-card from a world where fiction rarely lingers, at once a comic masterpiece and a study in national temperament that the doughtiest social historian would struggle to match.

D. J. Taylor
November 2015

Foreword

Book-writing can be a tedious job needing some incentive to keep one at it. The impulse here was 'can this unbelievable feat be made to sound like the truth even though it didn't happen?'

So I stacked the cards — a foreigner with remarkable theories, two young men with good reasons for having quit top-class football, a Chairman of napoleonic ability.

Then I dredged up memories of 1930 when I was an unqualified teacher, 18 years old and playing that single season for South Milford White Rose when we won a final which never ended. (Pitch invasion and furious fights are not new things.) I learnt much of rural life during that long-gone autumn, winter and early spring...

But is this story believable? Ah, it all depends upon whether you _want_ to believe it.

Jilean, 1992.

PART ONE

After the big Share-Out there was a thousand pounds left for an Official History. A top Sports Personality put the idea into our Chairman's head. His letter read, 'this most illustrious feat in modern Sporting Annals should – and must – be enshrined for posterity, and it will be my proud honour, sir, to perform this service for you and your gallant band, when suitable terms are agreed . . .' And he added that he would want Mr Fangfoss to write a short Foreword and that the frontispiece would be Mr Fangfoss's portrait in colour, over Mr Fangfoss's signature.

He was the man for the job; no doubt at all about that. His match reports in the quality Sunday press had really terrific quality. Even when the advertising and circulation managers relaxed their feud and plotted to dispatch him slumming up north to shiver through some dismal 4th Division brawl, you knew you were reading Literature. In fact, his descriptions were collected into books and put in the libraries and school anthologies. It was truly stupefying that, though he had heard of Mr Fangfoss, our Chairman had never heard of *him*.

'X?' he asked the Committee. 'X . . . who's he? You're the chap, Mr Gidner. Writing's your living.'

'Not like him,' I protested. 'What I write isn't real Writing . . .'

Mr Fangfoss's way of getting his way at meetings was invincible: he just changed the grammar and repeated himself in louder tones.

'MR GIDNER HERE'S THE CHAP. WRITING'S HIS LIVING. WE ALL KNOW THAT. All in favour say Aye . . . Unanimous! Very satisfactory! That's settled then. Five hundred down and five hundred when it's between covers. No airy-fairy stuff. Just stick to the unvarnished truth. And if you get stuck about what the truth was, have a word with me. Now the next business is . . .'

This isn't the Official History. It is only a rough sketch for it. The Official History will be much longer, every detail will be double-checked to make sure it is unvarnished truth, bad taste will be expunged, its Style is going to have more quality. It also will cost more.

But this will do nicely if all you want to know is what happened. And what happened happened because three – well, maybe four – remarkable men happened to be in the same spot at the same time. Just pure chance! Which, when you come to think about it, is why most unusual things happen. It boils down to this – THEY WERE THERE.

It all began on Friday, March 14th, the tag end of the previous football season. The time of the year, in our parts, when drains in the sugar-beet fields gulp out the last of the winter rains into ditches and then into dykes and the land again rises reassuringly above sea-level, the time when jam-jars fill up with sticky buds and, sure and certain harbinger of spring, council tenants who, later in the year, will be persecuted by the RDC for neglecting their front gardens, emerge cautiously and turn over a few optimistic spadefuls. And the village school had just suffered a government inspection. Not a casual look-over but a long lift of the lid and a cold-eyed scrutiny of the works. Alex Slingsby told me about it.

When it was all over, it seems this departing spy picked up his black briefcase, released a first smile and, half-way to the door, cautiously admitted that it had been a joy inspecting Dr Kossuth's little establishment and would that there were more like it in the land – but he wouldn't want to be quoted.

There was only one last trifling detail he must investigate. However had the Headmaster trained all, *all* the children, to perform such staggering feats of memorizing as he'd witnessed that week – e.g. the lad who'd recited two hundred lines of *How Horatius Kept the Bridge*, the small girl's awesomely exact description of a picture she'd seen on a class trip to Birmingham's Municipal Art Gallery, 'Chaucer Reading at the Court of King Edward III'. 'Her description of details of medieval dressmaking . . . quite astonishing! Why, I had to beg her to desist . . . ! What a demonstration of the dormant possibilities of human memory!'

Dr Kossuth was modestly gratified to hear this because, being a foreigner, he was not conditioned to our stony indifference to the education of the nation's young. He immediately expounded his Theory, the ins-and-outs of which I won't go into here (because this is about Football). But it came to this – Children need only to be taught How to Learn, and to remember what they learnt for only as long as the remembrance was of any earthly use. So each Steeple Sinderby child spent 7 ½ hours each week learning Exact Observation, Speed Reading, Knowledge Retention, and the bright ones got an important Extra – How to let Waffle wash over them whilst improving the time by thinking constructively.

'Mmmm . . . Ah-h-h,' the Government Inspector murmured, no doubt disturbed that, if this last revolutionary doctrine caught on, many such a one as he would want for bread.

'Anyway,' the Doctor went on, if it was Memorizing that had excited his distinguished guest's curiosity, then the two cases he had quoted were by no manner of means a true test of the

Kossuth Method, because (a) Horatius was a lively story and
(b) the girl *had* seen the picture. 'Pick any child,' he urged – *'Any*
child!' (The lot fell on Bill Fangfoss.) 'Now this little fellow has
not been on a train in his life, because Dr Beeching had pulled
up all the track in this county before he was born. Nevertheless, name but any railway in Britain known to you, even if it
survives only on maps, and Billy will recite its stations and
halts in exact order until he reaches a Main Line junction,
when you must tell him to turn either left or right or to go
straight on.'

'Banbury to Cheltenham,' the man said to Billy.

'Banbury – King's Sutton – Adderbury – Milton – Hook
Norton – Great Rollright – Chipping Norton – Kingham (for
Bledington and Church Icomb) – Stow on the Wold – Bourton
on the Water . . .'

'Thank you,' the Inspector said, 'and you are a smart little
chap and should pass the eleven-plus.'

And so the poor man went off, pondering this revelation of
how full many a gem of purest ray serene the caves of dark
unfathom'd Britain bear and, when round the first corner,
doubtlessly shook his head in humility at this encounter with a
Truly Great Mind.

The title of this story is not a snare and delusion: it *is*
about football. And I have related this incident only to show
that, unknown to Fame, in our village dwelt this man of
truly staggering originality, one ready, aye ready, to prise up
deeply embedded national institutions – even, as you will see,
those encrusted holy relics buried by Mr Hardaker and the
Football League – and to reshape them for this Day and
Age. Believe me, such men are thin on the ground in this once
great land.

But here he was. And, because he was here, Steeple Sinderby,
popn 547, height above sea-level in the Dry Season, 32 feet, won

Britain's premier sporting prize. Well, partly because he was here. There were others played a part. Even me.

It is sad to have to admit that Dr Kossuth was not a born Englishman. Because his political ideas had been as original as his educational ones, his Hungarian countrymen had taken away his university post and would have had his freedom also had he not left by the back door. And now he was content to live in peaceful obscurity and in our schoolhouse with roses round the door. His beautiful young wife also was a great consolation to him.

It was Philosophy he was doctor of – not Medicine. Actually, he put it about that he preferred 'Mr' so as to be spared being told about people's bad backs. But our Chairman, Mr Fangfoss, who was also the Chairman of the School Managers, insisted on him being addressed as 'Dr'. His two sons attended the village school, and Mr Fangfoss said that having a Dr as its headmaster was as good as sending them to private school; better, in fact, being on the rates.

It was only a small school and had a staff of three – the Doctor, Mr Croser, who'd been there man and boy as pupil, pupil-teacher and teacher, for sixty years, and Alex Slingsby. Everybody knows about him, *now* – he's football history, the Alexander the Great of the football compendia. And, for once, it isn't the usual puff: he *was* great. But, even on that fateful primogenital day, any fanatic who pores over soccer records like holy-writ might have told you that, seven years earlier, an A. Slingsby had played six games for Aston Villa before withdrawing into that vast and crowded silence which lies just off the sports-pages. Well, he had withdrawn to Steeple Sinderby where none guessed at this glory nipped in the bud, and where he ran the village side. He was now twenty-seven years of age.

The Wanderers had had a fairish season. They looked like

finishing third or fourth in the Barchester & District League and had survived to the semi-final of the Lord Channing Constituency Challenge Cup, before being cut to pieces by Cascob Colliery Welfare. Stirring around in these muddy shallows must have been painful for Alex, but he suffered in silence until . . . until the Government Inspector's wonder at the Doctor's System switched him from Branch to Main Line thinking.

He then said (and, for the Record, these are his *exact* words)

'If you gave your Full Mind to it, Doctor, I bet you could come up with something just as revolutionary for Football. And, if ever you do, I'd take it as a favour if you would let our Wanderers have first go at trying out whatever you come up with.'

It was a solemn moment. Later he admitted, 'It was as if another spoke – not me.'

'I'd like to help you, Mr Slingsby,' Dr Kossuth said. 'I'll think about it.'

Simple words but pregnant with meaning, as you will see.

I must now relate with some diffidence how I fitted into all this.

After I had this trouble and left theological college, I landed up in Sinderby, which, naturally, I'd never heard of before. I answered an advert offering two upstairs rooms rent-free in return for 'some help with an invalid during working hours'. This turned out to be no more than looking in now and then on Alex Slingsby's wife, Diana, to make sure she was all right. After what I'd been through, utter obscurity suited me down to the ground and, because my new job was one that can be done anywhere with a sub-post office, having no rent to pay made it just possible to keep my head above water. Believe me, writing verses for greetings cards isn't as easy as people imagine. I know that it's the picture that sells the card, but all except illiterates check on what's printed inside. There must be no hint of doubt about a Greeting Message; Sincerity and Truth with a bit of gloss on count above all with the customer. This may be why our Chairman, Mr Fangfoss, picked me to write the Official History; Mr Fangfoss venerates the Truth.

I was the Wanderers' Hon. Secretary. During the Season, I followed a regular routine. Monday evenings I devoted to administration. By this, I mean I posted off Saturday's result to our League Secretary, Mr H. Willis of Barchester, who in real life was the UDC rate-collector. Then I wrote a report for the *Barchester and District Weekly Messenger*, who paid me 50p plus postage, this being their flat rate whether they printed two lines or twenty. After this, I wrote out the team chosen for next week and took it to be pinned up in the Black Bull's window. Lastly, I took the dirty kit round to Mrs Lennox's for the wash (jerseys 2½ p, shorts 1p, ½ p a stocking – this included ironing the jerseys). If you are wondering how the team was picked, it was done whilst stripping after the match. It consisted of the captain yelling, 'Who can't turn out next week?'

I had one assistant – Corporal. He had been hit on the head at Alamein and had a silver plate there which he willingly showed those children who showed interest.

Saturdays were our big days. An hour before kick-off, I used to meet Corporal down by the Preaching Cross and we trudged up to the field, rigged up the nets, checked them for holes, hammered in the corner flags and redressed the touch-lines, centre-line, penalty areas etc. with sawdust. Then, whilst Corporal cleaned out blockages in the low-slung drain pipes that took off urine into a ditch and stopped up any gaps in the hedges through which lads could get in without paying, I cut up the half-time oranges in our converted LNER First Class coach. Always the same routine: it never varied.

J. L. Carr

Then I wrapped my martial cloak around me and huddled at the field-gate to sell admission tickets from a roll that already had lasted four years. About ten minutes before the whistle, I handed over to a boy and went across to the railway coach to knock down any stud-nails that had pushed through during the week and to rub in the embrocation. It was very important not to forget this last detail, because you always got the one or two players who were not above blaming their incompetent performances on not getting the rub.

From this, you will see that I did practically everything that had to be done for the club except kicking a ball. This is not self-pity. I liked the job (a) because it made something to do at the dead end of the week at the dead end of the year, and (b) because I like to feel indispensable. In these days, when everybody runs a mile to dodge involvement, this may sound a perversity. But it is a fact that there are people around who leave the district or this life and you don't even know they've gone. Then someone says, 'I've not seen X for a long time' and somebody answers, 'Oh, him! My wife read in the paper that he fell down dead somewhere. About last July. Or maybe it was his father . . .'

Well, if I'd fallen down dead, some Steeple Sinderby people would have known fast enough. Particularly if it happened in the football season and on either a Monday or a Saturday.

Thus, this voluntary exposure to the savagery of the climate and a minimum expenditure of lickspittle earned me a Place in local society; I was needed. Furthermore it dealt very satisfactorily with Saturday, Sunday and Monday nights when, as the great Tennyson says,

> . . . the nerves prick
> And tingle, and the heart is sick,
> And all the wheels of Being slow,

which anyone who has lived an unmarried life in lodgings in deep country will recognize as truth or, if anything, an understatement of it. People don't know about rural England between the last Mystery Autumn Foliage Coach Trip and the Mystery Blossom Journey into Spring. Mud, fog, dripping trees, blackness, floods, mighty rushing winds under doors that don't fit, damp hassocks, sticking organ keys, stone floors and that dreadful smell of decay.

Forgive this elaboration; I want to be *understood*. And if any reader is still wondering when the Football is going to start, then my time has not been wasted explaining what it takes to get twenty-two gladiators into the arena: he is hearing about football *now*.

On the following Saturday's home match, the Doctor arrived with Mrs Kossuth, his beautiful wife, who I shall describe. She was at least fifteen years younger than him, about my own age in fact, and I have been told she had been one of his undergraduate students in Hungary. Actually, she could only be described as breath-taking; anyway she took *my* breath away. Her silver-blonde hair was brushed straight back, her eyes were deep-set with an under-water look and her shape still makes me feel weak to contemplate. I had always thought very highly of English girls until I set eyes on Mrs Kossuth and, later, on a TV documentary which showed that every third young woman on the streets of Budapest was practically her double. In fact, I felt it wouldn't be all that disastrous if I *was* one of the Great Train Robbers (as I knew one or two locals said I was) and had to flee there as Mrs Kossuth had fled here.

On this particularly fine April day she was wearing her expensive leopard skin coat with a little fur hat perched on her heaped-up hair and long leather boots. And the Doctor was wearing a long black Central European overcoat with the astrakhan collar which marked him as having seen better days. Naturally, I refused to take their 5p admission.

If it seems that I have dwelt obsessively long on their appearance, it is only because the usual spectators at village matches are gross, bellicose women, whose aggression has been frustrated by their defeated husbands' flight to racing-pigeon lofts at the bottom of neighbours' gardens. And these women, summer and winter, wear garments suitable for life on an ice-floe, with several large buttons to hold them in.

When the game got under-way, the Doctor began talking discreetly into a mini-dictator – having first taken up a position in a remote corner of the ground, cleverly knowing that the English peasantry, with their long history of savagely put-down uprisings, are properly suspicious of records. And they left just before the end, the Doctor pausing to ask me to tell Alex Slingsby that he would see a professional game at Leicester before making a final appraisal. 'I count all this far beyond the call of duty, Mr Gidner,' he said. 'I mean paying money to look at grown men booting a ball about . . .'

Then, mercifully, he smiled.

Dr Kossuth came round to see us on the Tuesday evening after his trip to Leicester. He said this was very convenient because his wife was staying in London for the night with Hungarian friends. 'It is a club for the home-sick,' he said, 'where they talk over Old Times and dance mazurkas in their grandmammas' clothes. But that sort of stuff leaves me cold. I have signed papers to be an Englishman and one I mean to be. Now about this football game . . .'

And then followed the most startling exposition of the Art of the Possible I shall ever hear.

I will begin with the most astonishing product of his

king-sized brain. This was that, in his opinion, *there was very little difference between Leicester City and Sinderby Wanderers* or, for that matter, even our last week's opponents, Culverly Railway Sheds United. Apart from the same-sized field, the same rules and the same eleven men, the pattern of play was 90% the same too. 'Only 10% of it is different. You look dubious? Well, I have been studying English history. Yes, you see I have taken your request seriously, Mr Slingsby! Think about Hereford United.'

(We thought about them for a few solemn moments.)

The real differences were inconsiderable, he told us. The pitches in Big Time Football, being smoother, had a quite disproportionate effect on human control of a ball. He could not deny that the skill of the top league players was – well more skilful, but that was to be expected because they had been swept up from the four corners of the island plus Ireland. 'How really wasteful!' he kept repeating. 'These professionals chiefly are naturally clever young men who taught themselves against house-ends in the back streets. No one, but *no one* has taught them. But even so, they are not so different as all that from your own players. The striking difference is when the ball flies up into the air and needs redirection by the head . . .'

And then, for more than an hour, he went on, with Alex taking it down in a little red notebook. It took my breath away.

Then he bent forward and looked straight at Alex Slingsby. 'Yes,' he said (and smiled), 'I see that you are beginning to agree. You could match these expensive teams and you know you could. You personally, Mr Slingsby, I know, have this technical skill, but more than this, far, far more than this, you have the resolution. *You* could do it, all right. And what with one thing and another, my poor chap, you are in the right Frame of Mind. As your great Cromwell expressed it – in the bowels of Christ, you *know* these things could be brought to pass.'

He then sat back and listed calmly what later have become known as the Kossuth Postulations – the whole seven of them. And when he had done and had answered Alex's questions, he wrapped himself up in his Central European overcoat against the blast blowing in from his native steppes and said good-night. (There is a large painting of this historic moment in our Memorial Museum.)

As I have said, Alexander Slingsby was twenty-seven years of age. At seventeen, he had been like no other schoolboy foot-baller within fifty miles. Even then he had the lot – six feet two inches tall, bold and powerful as a lion and with a natural God-given way of gathering up the ball and, on the instant, moving off with it in immense strides. All this *and* intelligence. Yes – agreed – there are and always have been footballers simi-larly endowed. But he still had in hand one crowning talent vouchsafed to but few . . .

In cricket, a skipper is all: in soccer, he is no more than a name on the programme, his prime qualification being uni-versal amiability brought on either by a clouded intellect or the tongue-tie. Check with any manager who has drunk enough whisky to be truthful. With immense seriousness (*his* prime qualification) he will reply, 'Well, I suppose you are right but don't forget he must know how to spin a tenpenny-piece . . .'

Ah, but not so Slingsby. Even as his grammar school's cap-tain, he was a stripling Marlborough. Within ten minutes of kicking off he'd formed an opinion of the strength and weak-ness of the enemy and had set about blocking his side's own gaps and hammering away at theirs. And, from a mobile command-post, he had set up a chain of communication through two chiefs-of-staff, one up front, one in the backs. And this flow of informative exhortation went on till the final whis-tle, inexorably keeping his side's pattern of play in bewildering flux. It's commonplace now: they teach it at Sports Council coaching-schools. *But he invented it.* And one last attribute. Like Fluellen, that eminent 15th century Welsh striker, he properly set great store on 'the good order and disciplines ("Look you!") of the wars . . .'

When he left college he took up his first teaching post in Birmingham, and the Villa signed him as a part-time pro and, in fact, played him in six first-class games before his young wife, Diana, had her accident. Diana was Mr Croser's daughter and was a staff nurse at the Queen Elizabeth Hospital.

She was bicycling home through Digbeth, when a mad kid on a BSA rushed a halt sign and hit her. She was tossed head down against a sharp-edged kerb and was discharged from hospital a shocking wreck. At first, she tottered about in a jerking run, noticeably deteriorating month by month until, by this time, she no longer could walk nor talk and had to be carried everywhere, dressed, undressed, fed, washed, put on the toilet, cleaned-up – everything. By our rental arrangement, I looked in every hour to see if she was all right and, once each day, her mother came in to tidy around. But the burden was Alex's – cooking, washing, nursing. He never talked about it and abruptly rejected the doctor's suggestion that she should be put in a hospital. She used to be strapped to a wheeled-chair and lolled there, nodding away like a clockwork doll. Only her shining black hair recalled a lost loveliness. You had to make yourself think of her as 'Diana', and one awful character called her 'it'. But Alex was sure that she could understand what went on, always included her in the conversation and asked me to be kind enough to look in her direction now and then when we were talking. And, often, I used to hear him singing to her: he had a very good baritone voice. I particularly remember a few words of one song, so it must once have meant something to them . . .

'And then she went homeward, with one star awake,
As the swan in the evening moves over the lake . . .'

And this, of course, was why he'd abandoned his football at the Villa and had come to Steeple Sinderby so that she could be near her folks, and where he only had to slip across the road to see her each playtime. It will now be understood what Dr Kossuth meant with 'My poor chap – you are in the right Frame of Mind'.

When a lusty young chap is abruptly recast from lover to nurse, there's no telling what will happen. Many a civil rebellion or new religion has burst out from just such a ferment. In his bones Alex Slingsby knew that he was one of Nature's chosen. And that his home life had become a parched waste. So you might say that he was tinder-dry for the spark when it fell and blazed in him for those next few months. No doubt I shall be accused of poking into his private life: but this is the truth and Alex, looking back, will not want it suppressed.

There are two pubs in Sinderby – the Swan down by the ford and the Black Bull, near the Preaching Cross. This was the Wanderers' HQ . . . and I can best describe it by telling you that, now Sinderby is on the Map, university lecturers bring their history students during opening hours to study at first-hand living conditions in the Middle Ages. I don't wish to harp on the hardships of village life, but for the purposes of my story, you need to know that the Bull's Snug backed on to the landlord Mr Cory's foldyard where he wintered his beasts, and it was through this exit that he ejected any customer who overstepped his bounds of tolerance (which were very narrow indeed). And it was well known that, on moonless nights, you could blunder around amongst the bullocks and their droppings for quite a considerable time before finding the gate that let onto the highway. But we used the Bull as our HQ because Mr Cory let his back-room for meetings free of charge, so long as committee members took one round of drinks in with them and ordered another during the course of the evening. (All this of course, being highly personal, will be omitted from the Official History.)

It was a badly lit house, all the bulbs being of economic wattage. In fact, practically nothing had changed since the days when, it is said, Mr Cory's ancestors, displaying the same savage traits, trapped unwary travellers and slit their throats for as little as their watch-and-chain. And it was put about that there was a strayed Dutch seaman buried under the floorboards of the room where we held our meetings, and there undoubtedly was a most unusual smell. Though it could have been dry-rot.

We held our Annual General Meeting there at the end of April with our Chairman, Mr Arthur Fangfoss, presiding. Just a word or two about him.

Mr Fangfoss was not a follower of football; he never made any secret of this. In fact, as far as it is known, he had never watched a game, let alone played one. It is not that he actually disliked football: it was just an activity, like reading books, which he could live happily without. He was our Chairman because he was Chairman of everything else. You couldn't conceive of *any* Sinderby organization with anyone else in the Chair.

He was Chairman of the Rural District Council (his election address said simply, IF ELECTED I WILL KEEP DOWN THE RATES), Chairman of the Parish Council (no election was ever held), Chairman of the Parochial Church Council, the Grimsdyke Loaf Dole, the Allotment Association, the Bell Ringers Sociable, and the Old Folks Xmas Hamper & Coal Fund. He also was Chairman of the Constituency Conservative Party.

He was an extra large man and had an untrimmed drooping black moustache. He was also very rich and farmed 700 acres. His farmhouse, Howards End, was lapped in by fields of sugar beet and overfull dykes, and beyond it you eventually come to Middle Marsh unless you are drowned on the way.

He had two wives. The first, the legal one, Theresa, was elder sister to the second, who was simple and did all the rough work. Mrs Fangfoss proper was a smallish, clever woman who lived mostly in the front room, where she wrote always one and sometimes two romance books each year. While her sister kept to the scullery and kitchen and was big and strong and very amiable. I have always been given to understand that Mrs Fangfoss did not object to her husband's arrangement with her sister, because it gave her more time for authorship. Her only proviso was that he did it outside the house itself and, as farms have many cosy corners in granaries and barns, with plenty of straw and sacks around, this was no great hardship. The younger sister had two children by Mr Fangfoss, but they were brought up as her own by Mrs Fangfoss, and it was locally acknowledged with wonder that they took after her in looks. She referred to her more fruitful sister as Poor Beatie and the boys called their true mother Auntie. This is not so unusual as you might suppose in the country, where Auntie or Uncle has several meanings in addition to those in the *Shorter Oxford*.

This unusual situation suited Mr Fangfoss very well and kept him in a good humour; in fact, I think it explained his utter lack of irritability and his calmness of mind and why he was much more charitable than the rest of us. I have read that travellers along the Congo come away with similar impressions of the much married native chiefs there. Later on, a very well-known TV personality, having failed to cheekily drag out Mr Fangfoss's private life and parade it before the viewers, scoffed at him, implying that he was a simple peasant. But it was plain that he was envious of his simplicity.

Now back to the AGM.

I enjoy AGMs because I like writing minutes and, even more, reading them aloud. Everybody has a creative urge and likes to exhibit what he has created for the admiration of others and, if you are secretary of any sort of club, you can read aloud what you have written and people have to listen. No one can really complain about its length because accurate detail is extremely important and, if you take care to keep mentioning people's names, 'Mr X said' or 'Mr Y demurred', they pay attention, because everybody likes his name mentioned as add-itional confirmation that he is alive.

When I'd read the minutes at this particular AGM and then the correspondence, the same committee as last time was elected en bloc. (In a village, you avoid having elections to save hurting feelings and rely on death or flittings for welcome changes.)

The proposal that we enter the FA Cup Competition was down in the name of Alex and the Revd Giles Montagu seconded it.

Mr Fangfoss forestalled any objection on account of the high £100 entry fee by declaring it would be his pleasure to stump up from his own pocket, though he didn't want anybody to think farmers had had a good year, but as his elder boy had passed the eleven-plus he had great confidence in Mr Slingsby, and, if he thought we should make a splash in the football world, well he would cough up, particularly as this was his twenty-fifth year in office as Chairman. He tactlessly added that he didn't suppose we'd get any further than the district qualifying first round but it was 'better to have played and lost than never to have played at all'. He requested that this last remark should be recorded in full in the minutes.

'It'll be a bit of a laugh in the neighbourhood when they hear about it,' said Fred Bleasby. 'I mean us going in for the FA Cup, particularly this year when the top Scots clubs are coming in for the first time . . .'

'The same sort of folks laughed at Noah,' Mr Fangfoss said. He then closed the meeting.

Did you ever hear of the great John Nyren (1724–1787), who kept the village pub, the Bat & Ball, on Halfpenny Down in Hampshire, and who ran the local cricket club in the glorious Dawn of that game? He recruited ten others – bright and illustrious now in the Annals but, then, following obscure ways and quite unknown to fame – Silver Billy Beldham, John Willis, who made the giant evolutionary stride from underarm to round-arm bowling (and, like Galileo, suffered for it), and David Harris, whose underarms were so venomous that even long-stop on the boundary wore a sack of hay. Reflect also on James Aylward, farm labourer, who scored 177 against All-England when the village beat them in 1787. And, believe me, All-England was no push-over with opening batsmen like Lord Frederick Beauclerk, who reposed such confidence in his defensive play that he used to hang a valuable gold watch from his stumps, and the Yorkshire hunting squire, Mr Osbaldiston, who is reported – even in Lancashire – to have batted better on four legs than normal man does on two.

But this Nyren, this simple inn-keeper, had so much faith in his skill and power that, in one rare lapse into immodesty, witnesses report him remarking, 'I suppose that if I was to *think* every ball, depend upon it, t'other side 'd never make one run between 'em.' And, after his men had made 405 (all run, no boundaries), he took up his fiddle and began where he'd left off on a Bach partita . . .

Well, divided by the centuries, Alex Slingsby was a blood-brother to that man. Like this Nyren, Alex drove his will deep into all we did; he planned and he made his plans work and anyone who got in his way was trodden under. With the hind-sight that all minor prophets need, I now see that, right from that AGM, he believed that he could shake Football to its very foundations and thereafter bent his mind to this praiseworthy task.

First, he chose four players from the Sinderby side, five others from similar farming villages and four from Cascob, a colliery side famed locally for their unexampled savagery, foul language and iron constitutions. Then, one by one, he visited these men in their own homes and persuaded them to throw in their lot, all or nothing, for the coming season. He lacked only a goalkeeper. Remember this last point; I shall be coming back to it.

Then he gathered together this motley band and explained to them Kossuth Postulation No. I, which was a theory of ball control. It was not completely original because Alex said that, in his youth, he had seen a great player demonstrating it, per-haps not even knowing that it was the secret of his strength – the great Wilfred Mannion, who graced an England side twenty-six times. Yet nobody seems to have analysed what made Mannion beyond compare. If this sounds unlikely when half-a-million fans watch games weekly, you have to remember that, unlike cricket audiences, by and large, football supporters are not creatures of intellect but of emotion.

POSTULATION ONE

Surely it is possible to move a ball without staring down at your feet. Women don't watch their hands when knitting.

These simple words struck the chosen few like a great beam of searching light and, all that summer, you could see them running round Mr Fangfoss's meadow practising it. Initially, ball and man pursued contrary courses but, by mid-June, I was astonished to see Alex, Giles Montagu and Billy Sledmer had somewhat more than a clue, marvelling at the rare pleasure of watching anguished faces close-up, as they slipped past. It was no more than logic to the Doctor, but it was magic to them. The rest of the side never really got hold of it and would only risk it very occasionally but, even so, when it came off, it was devastating.

POSTULATION TWO

A very good goalkeeper is a team's most valuable asset. Almost alone he can thwart superior opponents.

POSTULATION THREE

A goalkeeper does not need to be an accomplished footballer. He needs qualifications similar to a good cabinet-maker or bus driver – distinguishing instantly what will or will not fill a space. To this must be allied outstanding agility and courage.

Was there such a one in our district? Certainly no one playing football in our League fitted this description. So Alex Slingsby's father-in-law, Mr Croser, who had unrivalled knowledge of local genealogy, was consulted. He sucked his pipe and sat back, gazing through steel-rimmed spectacles deep into the past. Then he said, 'Monkey Tonks! His dad was Joe Tonks, who married Annie Snow, and *her* mother was brought up in a travelling circus and performed on the trapeze. His real name is Alfie. He got the "Monkey" from the other lads – at nine years of age he didn't *climb* trees, he *ran* up them. When he was fifteen he could ride as fast with his back to the handlebars as most youths do right way round. And before he was twenty, he ascended the church steeple without scaffolding to straighten the weathercock after a gale.'

Even *thinking* about deeds this Child of Nature had dared and done made me sweat with terror. But, remarkably, one thing is undisputed and must be recorded – until his hour of glory came he had avoided all ball games like the plague – he said they were too *childish*.

Alex Slingsby was not one for mass exhortation. He took a man off on his own and, when he'd finished, that man had a mission and knew that Slingsby's particularly beady eye would be on him to see that he pursued it.

So, by the time he had finished with Monkey, that person had put away spectacular feats on bike, branch and steeple and freely acknowledged that, deep in the womb of Time, it had been ordained that, after earning his daily bread as the proprietor of a rural milk-round, his part in the Scheme of Things was to foil attempts to get a ball past him. Thenceforward, all was grist to his mill and he recruited all comers to shoot balls at him. In fact, it was reported that he compelled one large strong family to pay off unpaid milk bills thus in their own back garden. Hour after hour, evening after evening throughout that summer, he leapt, grovelled and dived, frustrating the passage of balls. It had become a way of life to him and his reflexes became radar sharp. It was plain that the only balls likely to squeeze past Monkey would have to be bullocked through or pumped in at point-blank range or deflected from geometric law by intruding knees, necks or backsides.

It could be said with utter truth that A. Tonks was Postulations Two and Three made flesh. But I hope he won't mind it being suggested that, to the end, he never understood football or really cared for it. He just liked stopping balls and, like empty milk-bottles, returning them for further consumption.

Alex Slingsby brooded long on the Doctor's 4th Law. 'He's right,' he said to me as we sat over our baked beans on toast and cocoa, now and then breaking off to give Diana a spoonful. 'As usual,' he added. 'As usual as what?' I asked. 'The Doctor's right as usual,' he said. 'Puts his finger right on it every time. Genius!'

POSTULATION FOUR

The only truly striking difference between the technical skills in amateur and professional players is the latter's control of a ball's movement when struck by his head.

Recommendations. (1) Whenever possible, keep the ball close to the ground and (2) select terrain disadvantageous to flighted passage of balls.

Yes, of course. Obviously! This was Alex Slingsby's chief fear – the dreaded head-blows from crosses and corners professionals are so skilled at. And the only serious practice we were going to get in combating them would be in games, each of which might be our last if we didn't learn fast enough. However, the Doctor's Recommendation No. 2 seemed to offer some slight hope of salvation, so we asked him about it.

'I am afraid,' he said, 'alas, I am truly afraid that there is no succour to be had on *their* grounds. But, playing at home . . . ah, that is a very different matter.' And he smiled faintly.

'In military engagements, a choice of terrain has ever been a chief consideration,' he said. 'At Bannockburn, the Scots cunningly pocked the field with hidden pits and, at Waterloo, you will recall that your Wellington made the French play uphill both halves. Thus, you must re-site your pitch to one that is as dissimilar as possible from anything a professional can have played on since he left his school playground. If the surface-excellence of Wembley has a quotient of 100, your midden (the right word?) must be no more than 15 points on the same scale.

'Have no pricks of conscience,' he went on. 'The English are properly honoured amongst Europeans for their protestations of uprightness whilst preparing the destruction of their enemies. And one more detail . . . choose a field so small that your opponents cannot pack in more supporting Noise than you yourselves can muster. And, because Sinderby will be invaded by great hordes, you must find a field with strong natural defences.'

Ah, what a remarkable man he was!

So we co-opted Mr Fangfoss and plodded over every enclosure in the parish big enough to hold posts and pitch until, after much heart-searching too, we made a unanimous choice of Parson's Plow. This was glebe meadow, rented out for grass-keeping to augment the living of our right-wing, the Vicar, Revd Giles Montagu. Denying its name, it had not been ploughed in living memory. Like that famous ground at Margate it had a steep slope, not from end to end but from side to side. Its only drawback was an ancient oak standing close to the centre-spot.

'This is the Promised Land!' Alex exclaimed. 'And it does not need the confirmation of a burning bush. Anything flying in from the high side will sail above even the most catlike noddy and, from below, anything meant for heads will arrive only chest-high. But look at that tree!'

'There's a Ministry of the Environment Preservation Order on that there oak,' Mr Fangfoss told us. 'But, as Chairman of the Parish Council, I'll declare it dangerous, which it would be if run into. So, if the Vicar don't mind, I'll have it out and, when the roots wither, ground'll sink. And then, there's pog end. Don't forget pog end. There's an old spring deeper 'n any drain and you'll find falling balls won't bounce and running balls'll dra-a-ag.' He then added unnecessarily, 'There'll be no need to record what I've said in the minutes, Mr Gidner.'

So we gazed and wondered at the Marvels of Nature.

The Doctor brought us down to earth. 'Yes,' he said, 'but oh be warned. Your pitch could well be your fortune, but only if you win on it. Don't give them a second chance. You might as well lose as draw and have to play away. Remember Hereford!'

And we stood again in reverent silence and remembered Hereford.

But still – how could we do it? How could we possibly do it? How could we match a mob of milkmen, farmers, the parson and a job-lot of pit-men from Cascob Main against Big Business whose performers had cost the Mint?

And at the next meeting, after I'd read the minutes, I took a deep breath and said this in an unnaturally loud voice, prefacing it with 'Mr Chairman . . .'

'When I was nobbut a lad in the Sunday-school we had a hymn,' Mr Fangfoss said. 'Would you care to know what it was, Mr Gidner?'

I could have sunk through the floor and joined the buried sailor.

'As I recall the wording of it, the chorus ran

> Trust and Obey
> For there's No Other Way.

Now, Mr Slingsby,' he went on briskly, 'you said you were going to discuss the Doctor's next little hint.'

POSTULATION FIVE

Every player except the centre-forward must defend his own goal, and every player except the goalkeeper must assault his opponents' goal.

As this message fermented in our minds, we sat in awed silence, the duller ones stupefied and the more imaginative ones reeling at the thought of all the thundering up and down and round and round that would have to be done. 'Talk about Nelson's Men of Iron!' Giles Montagu said.

'Exactly!' said Alex. 'Can *anyone* dispute that our only hope to cope with good-class professional teams is to be as fit as them. And fitter, because we'll just have to keep working when they want to knock off. Have you ever watched a long-distance runner get a new access of speed as he nears the post? Yet he must have been just as tired as he was a quarter of a mile back. Have you felt strength inject itself into your vitals when danger stares you in the face? Let me explain. I was once walking with Diana by a river bank, and a great swan in an excess of uxoriousness began to hiss, lowered its head flat on its back and swam like a warship at me. My first instinct was to take flight but suddenly – and I was very tired because my wife was a great walker – I felt a stiffening of my sinews and a primeval urge to rush at that swan and tear it apart like Samson tore the lion . . .' He didn't finish the story because he could see he'd made his point and, like too few propagandists, recognized where an irrelevance begins.

The more intelligent players were entirely convinced. And those that weren't, plainly didn't like the look in his face and gladly professed conviction also.

As we separated homewards, Mr Fangfoss caught up with me. 'Words are your living, Mr Gidner,' he said. 'Tell me – "uxorious" – now what is its meaning?'

Well, naturally I knew, because they used to warn us against it at theological college. But, of all people, how could I tell *him*?

Mercifully Giles Montagu overheard.

'"Husbandry" . . . right in your own way of business, Mr Fangfoss,' he said. 'In a roundabout way, as you might say.'

From that day on, I listened to our Vicar's sermons with closer attention.

★

As I have said, the sports writers later dubbed him 'Alexander the Great'. But I don't think for a minute that they realized that he actually *was* great. As a measure of the man, consider this – he talked all players and committee members into arranging their summer holiday into a training camp at Snainton-on-Sea.

There was some grumbling from wives who preferred a normal holiday on the Bingo Belt to Snainton's one pub, a sub-post office shop and buses taking a roundabout route to Yarmouth three times a week. *But they came.* All but George Grindle. He was our best forward and had joined us the year before from Barchester City, with whom he'd had a row. He had scored 34 goals and had brought with him his personal fan club of Maisie Twemlow and four or five other maniacs. 'Come on, George!' they used to scream. Not 'Come on, Sinderby!' I didn't care greatly for him. He wanted the Big Shot treatment, expecting *me* to rub in his liniment. He made sure that we understood he was doing us a favour turning out. And on wet Saturdays sometimes he didn't. But, like chumps, we still picked him next week. Well, George snarled that no one was telling him where he'd spend his holidays. And off he went to the Costa del Sol, all expenses paid by a Barchester building contractor to solace his only daughter.

'Right,' said Alex. 'Send him this letter and Mr Fangfoss will sign it.'

Dear George,

The Club is disappointed that you cannot go with us to training camp. However, as the Committee regard this as vital for physical fitness and team-spirit, we regret to tell you that your membership has been terminated. Thank you for your highly valued past services.

This was revolutionary. Any minor league secretary will tell you that. I mean no village ever dares sack amateur footballers or, for that matter, amateur anybodies. It can never have happened to George before and I gather the sun didn't shine so bright on his girl friend at the Costa. And to rub it in, I was asked to discreetly leak it around what had happened. *'Pour encourager les autres,'* said Mr Fangfoss, who was picking up a few such prestige phrases from his son, who, as the inspector had prophesied, had newly gone to Grammar School.

This thunderbolt was reported to a committee meeting as a *fait-accompli* (Mr Fangfoss) and they were asked to endorse it. As all committees are clay in the hands of determined men who fix agendas, they did. And there was a letter from Maisie Twemlow, who had found out about George's companion and now committed her fan club to our support. This news item was received with dismay.

'What are we going to do without him?' I asked Alex as we came away. 'He's our only real goal-grabber.'

'Haven't the faintest,' he said. 'Nothing else we could do though, was there?'

'Well . . .' I said doubtfully. He then informed me that, in similar situations in the past, he'd received Guidance, so I let it drop. And, as it happened, this Guidance came towards the end of summer, at Snainton-on-Sea itself.

For five days all the men except Mr Fangfoss (although he had brought only his first wife) ploughed up and down the sandhills. These are a geological phenomenon in Western Europe, because the sand is so fine your foot goes in six inches and you have to drag it out with one and sometimes two hands before you can move on. Gradually everybody became so strong doing this that most of us could do a half-mile in a sort of stagger without stopping. Also, as there is always a freezing blast blowing at Snainton, no one could loaf for more than two or three minutes, and thus we lived tremendously healthy lives, grudgingly admitting we'd never felt better.

When, at the end of the sixth day, Alex announced that the rest of the week was Free, we all went by bus to Yarmouth, where the world began again. There, as two or three of us were fighting our way against a gale blowing along the Prom, we saw a small crowd gathered around a speaker on a box who was going on at them. 'Oh dear,' said Giles Montagu (the Vicar I mentioned earlier), 'it is Biddy, I'm afraid.'

I shall have to explain about Biddy. To begin with, she was Giles's only sister and kept house for him, and, like Mrs Kossuth, she was a beauty of the first order, having raven-black hair, flashing eyes and a marvellous bust. Outrageously, she despised these gifts from the gods and, instead of adorning them suitably with exotica from doll-boutiques, she threw on whatever happened to be lying on the bedroom floor. But even clad in muddy shoes, a torn tweed skirt, grubby shirt-waister and a plastic red rain-hat, her essential glory shone through.

Now you would expect anyone brought up in a parsonage to be biased towards religion. It would be unnatural if it was otherwise. And so it was with Biddy. Whilst still at boarding school she had put aside the Faith of her Fathers and had become a Jehovah's Witness. Since all Anglicans know theirs is the true faith, they don't go around stuffing it down other people's throats, feeling it enough to slide into their little boxes to mutter pleas for the defence in Tudor English and to squeeze a cold smile at whoever they happen to pass in the porch on their way back to the rest of the week. Not so a Witness, who is expressly charged to save all men from the furnace. However, Biddy, having quickly picked up the nicer points of proselytizing exhortation, soon fell out with the JW and founded her own Religion (which I shall touch on later), preaching it with the frightening zeal and power that come of knowing you are right.

So you might meet Biddy in any of six or seven surrounding parishes pushing an old pram half full of badly duplicated leaflets, peddling her wares and message to embarrassed householders, sparing neither cottage nor hall, ambushing householders with glittering eye, while kitchens filled with the smoke of charring dinners.

As we could see that Giles was embarrassed we didn't probe closer but observed from a distance. Behind, she had a banner, 'REPENT – THE DAY COMETH', left over from her Witness days and, before, a huddle of six men and two little girls. The men were middle-aged refugees from the flat horror of hearth and home, marvelling that such beauty could be seeking to solicit their immortal souls. They plainly were not absorbing her philosophical argument. This was not because of mental incapacity: Biddy's panting magnificence was such that, like a spider, she drugged her victims and immobilized their minds. When I first came to Sinderby I fell in love with Biddy and thought at last I had solved my trouble. Until she turned on me one single pulverizing blast – 'What *you* need is Purpose. You lack *Purpose*! Come back when you've found some!'

And it was true: I *do* lack Purpose.

So we watched. 'You know, Giles,' Alex said ruminatively, 'your sister has extraordinary potential. Any young woman who has the stamina to push a pram the weight of three babies and the constitution to stand still in this wind and be heard above it, the zeal to seek to strike fire in England's stony heart and the fanatic blindness to believe that she *can* . . . that person can do *anything*. Now we must consider how we can enlist her quite exceptional talents . . . for Biddy is one of Sinderby's assets . . .'

'I'm afraid Biddy has been going her own way since the

cradle,' said poor Giles, 'but I know what you mean. From her age of fourteen our doorstep has been littered with suitors. Some have loved her body and some her brain, but none ever succeeded in converting either to his own ends.'

'There is a key to every door,' said Alex. 'It's really a matter of recruiting Biddy's help without her knowing it, and this I believe I can do, as I have just had a hint of the Guidance I have been expecting daily.'

No more than three miles from Sinderby, lost in the fenland, was Middle Marsh and there, rotting gently away, dwelt the great Sid Swift, the Shooting Star himself. As every true fan remembers, he had that one terrific season (52 goals) in the First Division. Then utter silence. Like a rocket – whoosh, roar, cascade, then blackness as though it had never been. He was not the first. Where do they go? Just think of cricket and football stars that disappear! Opening the innings for England one season; then gone. And perhaps years later, you read in the papers that he's died and you think, 'Good God, fancy that! The great X gone! I'd completely forgotten him!' Or worse – 'Good heavens . . . was he still alive!'

Anyway, I can tell you what happened to Sid Swift. Not strong drink like many a great player: just common melancholia . . . and, unbelievably, caught overnight. He went trustingly to bed like anyone might, success and prosperity stretching confidently before him; yet awoke next day finding no purpose in Life, no pride in Action, no joy in Fame. And to a non-literate person who has never had to reflect on the Purpose and Meaning of life in order to pass in Eng. Lit., this was a severe shock indeed. Like most disasters, there was no explaining it. One can only say, 'It happened.'

Over that sad breakfast, he is supposed to have asked his widowed mother if she truly believed that he had been sent into this world just to boot a ball around whilst a maddened mob poured noise over him. It was indeed a solemn thought and this I can understand. Mercifully, most of us are spared such spiritual inquests.

With hindsight, she immediately should have sought pastoral aid from Giles Montagu, who had played in the Winchester College XI, or, considering Sid's eminence, a sporting bishop who could have been counted on to reassure him that to blast spectacular goals was indeed God's Will. But his mother was a poor old country woman, a chapel-goer reared to speak only what she believed to be true. So she answered, 'I don't know, Sidney: I really don't know. God moves in a mysterious way. Tha must make up thi own mind, lad.'

So he was compelled to *think* and this is unnerving if you're not used to it. The only thing a football player should think about is football and how to obtain maximum remuneration for performing it.

And thus the Slide began. From the First Division to the Midland League wilderness within six weeks! At the end of the season, a flabbergasted Board of Directors foreclosed his contract, sadly gave him an automatic electronic gold wristwatch, wished him well and asked if he would like to be put on their Free Transfer List. But, rather than suffer this last indignity, he just disappeared. And when he disappeared off the sports pages too, he became officially deceased.

I suppose it was a sort of specialized breakdown, because he wouldn't get dressed of a morning nor shaved, nor would he leave the house or meet anybody or go to a specialist or let anyone try to do anything for him. Fortunately he wasn't married and they scraped along on his mother's widow's pension. All that was three years ago and there he was, lying like a nugget of purest gold on our doorstep.

*

The Revd Giles Montagu, MA, played football like a scene from the *Magnet*: he was all that the Greyfriars Ist XI would have hoped for. He streaked along his wing in great cavalierish curves and charged heartily shoulder to shoulder in antique style. But, back at work and on his parish rounds, he was so earnest he felt that he *had* to talk religion and, as most of his flock were quite unable to keep going on this topic for more than a couple of minutes, there were agonized silences during which both parties prayed for deliverance. In fact, I was told that empty-headed newlyweds, seeing him approach, would fling themselves on the floor behind the sofa and lie giggling in each other's arms until the knocking stopped.

As may be gathered from his belief in Guidance, Alex was a hard-line Baptist, but Diana was C of E, so Giles went in on Mondays and Fridays to administer holy communion to her. This done, he made it his business to sit for at least an hour; on Mondays he read her his sermon and on Fridays gave her a detailed assessment of the spiritual state of his parish. That she was unable to comment seemed to encourage him. And, as this was whilst Alex was in school, his visits were highly appreciated.

So, on Wednesdays and after church on Sundays, Giles was made very welcome to supper, whilst we talked soccer or cricket according to the season. Thus, it must have seemed quite natural in the week after our return from Snainton, for his host to say, 'What about Sid Swift?'

And, whilst Giles was aglow with the remembrance of this dead-to-the-world hero, he was asked firmly why Biddy couldn't do something about him when she called around Middle Marsh with her tracts? Football, of course, must not be mentioned to him. All that was needful was that she should implant *Purpose* into Sid. It would then follow that he would want to retrieve his true place in Society, which was to shoot goals with unparalleled force and direction. Alex's last words to him on the doorstep were, 'Vicar, just think of Sid Swift's head picking up one of your right crosses.' Just think . . . it was enough to give any winger hysteria.

When I write this up as Official History I naturally shall speculate at length on what went on between brother and sister, and it must have been agonizing because Biddy had more guile in her little finger than Giles had in his head, although I heard him swear (with sweat starting from his brow at the memory of it) that he had *not* mentioned football and that he'd stuck to *Purpose*. Over the years, I have given some thought to this vital happening, and I have now come to the one sensible conclusion that Biddy saw through his pitiful plot and decided to fall in with him simply to reassure herself that she was on top of her self-appointed mission to mankind. Well, we all have our professional pride . . .

As I have said, she already was well in with Sid's mother, who had joined her Religion, so Biddy couldn't be put off like the neighbours, by being told that her son was upstairs studying for the Open University. So he was lured into her presence.

The cure was near enough instantaneous. He looked on the Prophet's lovely face and form and *knew* from a stirring in his soul and elsewhere that life indeed had very exciting Purpose. And she looked at him with burning eyes and knew that she had found a disciple prepared to follow unswervingly to whatever goal she led.

The upshot of all this was the astonishing sight of the Shooting Star pushing Biddy's pram around the countryside and his instant resurrection to the land of the living. If there was any doubt at all about his conversion, it was silenced one Saturday night in Cascob when the pubs threw out and two drunken pit-men, shouting blasphemy at Biddy on her box, were struck down as dead by thunderbolts directed by Sid with something more like pagan ferocity than Christian humility.

Soon after this, the school caretaker fatally drove his motor-scooter into a dyke and Mr Fangfoss, as Chairman of the Managers, appointed Sid in his place. He was then shown a football as a bloodhound is shown a smell and, from deeply rooted habit, struck it a violent blow with his foot into the school coke-heap, which disintegrated, showering volcanic ash on the gravestones just over the wall.

He began training that same evening.

I have now described my dramatis personae – Dr Kossuth and his beautiful wife, Alex Slingsby and Diana, poor creature, Mr Fangfoss and his two wives, the devastating Biddy – and the Shooting Star himself. And now I feel it quite proper to briefly set the stage itself, i.e. Steeple Sinderby & District.

To tell truth, there isn't much to tell. Our district lies in a landscape neither charming nor downright ugly; it grows on you and, after a while, you don't notice it. Professor Pevsner had so low an opinion of what he found that he described the village as a 'settlement' –

St Bartholomew. Dec. but much worked-over by Butterfield in 1847. Disproportionately large tower and spire rebuilt 1883 after collapse. On S. wall 14th century cross sawn in half. An inn, the Black Bull, hints of a 15th century core.

But Arthur Mee gives us much more space. It is too long to quote in full, though it will be in the Official History and, like I plan that to be, is quality prose. –

We see its age old spire far away as we wend our way across this pastoral, watered landscape, its hedges ablaze with wild roses of every hue, the air laden with the song of birds. Its churchyard is crowned with the sombre glory of a stately cedar of Lebanon and under its spreading boughs the good folk of the village have been summoned by bells for countless generations, till at last they rest beneath its evening shade . . .

The architectural features which Professor Pevsner passed over are the British Legion Club, the Swan Inn, the Primitive Methodist Chapel (now the Cup Final Memorial Museum) and the Preaching Cross (of which only a largish stone remains).

The village plan is simple: there are two streets, one called Front Street and the other Back Lane. Back Lane doesn't go anywhere but you can get back to Front Street by either Bake-Oven Ginnel, Gun Passage or Ladd's Yard. Front Street dwindles off past the Preaching Cross before petering out in Swanpasture, which leads into Rushypasture. Beyond that, there is a cart-track to Mr Fangfoss's farm, known locally as Towlers End but renamed Howards End by Mrs Fangfoss. This is local brick, three storeys, very plain, relieved above the door with the other half of the Janus cross (see Pevsner).

Beyond that there are just fields, and I once asked our Chairman what lay beyond those fields and he said, 'More'.

Our principal product is sugar beet, which is a sort of large parsnip. You can't eat it but, when chewed up by machinery, it yields sugar. It comes to maturity after corn harvest and fills in time-sheets between then and Christmas. The climate is typically English, but more so in January and February, when the district soaks up rain like a sponge and biting winds blow in from the USSR. Over the centuries this has developed the local characteristic of emitting talking sounds through shut teeth.

Nothing in history has ever happened here except the steeple falling down during the night of Jan. 28th, 1884 – not 1883 as Professor Pevsner states – and the Dutch sailor getting his throat cut. Arthur Mee touches on Thomas Dadds, the

Peasant Poet (May 20, 1841 – June 13, 1884), who was Sexton and Verger. You may not have heard of him since he is never included in school anthologies, but he is highly thought of in Sinderby & District and, on his birthday, the school-children strew flowers on what is said to be his grave – poetry being then, as still, a poor-paying job, so he didn't leave enough for the purchase of a headstone.

There are a lot of Daddses still around and – this is very interesting – a direct descendant of the poet, 'Bosey' Dadds, is still in charge of the church stove, it being a hereditary office handed from one Dadds to the next. In fact, there are several references to it (the stove) in Thomas Dadds's Works. For example,

> And here I dwell, stranger to Fame
> Yet Keeper of the Sacred Flame . . .
> *(Meditations on Obscurity)*

and

> Let others sport in Sappho's Grove
> Enough for me to tend this stove.
> *(Reflections on Fame)*

Actually, being in the same line of business, I am doing a monograph on him with an eye to academic publication. To date, he has not been discovered by American post-graduates on Foundation Grants so I have the monopoly of him.

PART TWO

And so the summer turned towards its end, a season of warm, sanguine weather and the start of a new football season. For our first game our side was as follows,

A. Tonks, G. H. Hardcastle, F. Ormskirk, A. J. Crummock,
A. Slingsby, F. Maidstone, R. S. G. Montagu, J. Midgely,
S. Swift, R. W. Hutton, W. Sledmer.

But no sooner were the names pinned up in the Bull window than our only near-mutiny was brought on by the new all-buttercup-yellow strip, which had been chosen by Alex after he'd read that the Royal National Lifeboat Institution's researches showed this colour to be most visible in rough dark seas and, thus, mud. They looked at it with horror – shirts, shorts, stockings, all this one sickly hue. Then, before the first protesting cry, mercifully it began to rain. And, after Mrs Lennox's first wash, no garment was ever itself again: the crisis passed.

The opposition was North Baddesley Congs (Congregational Chapel), and for what transpired I have a cutting from the *East Barset Weekly Messenger*, written up by their staff reporter, Alice (Ginchy) Trigger, who did funerals, inquests, weddings, council meetings and all sport. She was seventeen with an open, truthful face, believing eyes and wore a leather rig-out that creaked. She sped from happening to happening on her Yamamoto, closing with her quarry, ballpoint poised and 'You were saying?' on her lips. Her heroes were Thomas Hardy and Monty Python.

CONGS CATASTROPHE

In their primal gladiatorial tourney N. Baddesley jousting on their own bailiwick encountered the full and furious blast of Steeple Sinderby's New Look Lads spearheaded by Sid Swift, long-lost Shooting Star idol of Brum fans a handful of time ago. The Ringers clocked up eleven strikes and only the inexorable march of time muffled a full peal of twelve.

Goals – Swift (8) Slingsby (2) Montagu (1)

The second fixture was v. Hackthorn Young Conservatives, who turned up one man short and asked would we mind if a girl supporter filled in. As is well known, these daughters of the soil are more formidable than their menfolk, but the ref said that there didn't seem to be any rule prohibiting mixed-sex sides so she could play. However, he added that he would get such a rule inserted at the next league meeting. Once more, I quote Ginchy Trigger –

HACKTHORN AMAZON SUBDUED

Initiating the virgin turf of Parson's Plow, FA Cup contenders, Sinderby Wanderers, were in scintillating form and by half-time had netted seven. That they did not encore this in the second session was because all eleven Hackthorners crammed their own area and, with great courage, blocked their bailiwick with backs, heads, chests and, from piercing shrieks of agony, I diagnose other things. Dolly Preston subbed for Jeremy Hope-Bowdler, who was a handsome best man at his personable cousin Henry Willerby's wedding to lovely Jane Hurstly-Smith at St Mary's, Romanby – see p. 7. After the game I found her sobbing as she struggled back into her slimline Antarex skirt and trench coat. 'Nine to Nothing is so shame-making a beating,' she told me.

There had been quite a lift of interest in the village after our away win at Baddesley and this was reflected in the gate. At our first home game last season I took 25 pence. This time it was 70 pence.

And so we come to the First Qualifying Round of the Football Association's Challenge Trophy, the FA Cup. Initially, this is played off in regions to save travelling expenses, and we had been told to play the only other competitor in our county, i.e. Barchester City (known locally as the Holy Boys).

Barchester has a cathedral and, until they built the Discount Hyper-Market, this was its biggest attraction. On fine Saturdays the City draws about 250 paying spectators, augmented by between 20 and 30 Pensioners who are driven out for air from the Cathedral Almshouses by the Warden Canon. But, in cold, wet weather, they get no more than 70 or 80 – including the full tally of Pensioners – all huddled in their 'grandstand', which is very interesting architecturally because it tones in with the Cathedral and is the only football building mentioned in Professor Pevsner's *Buildings of England*.

They have one part-time professional by arrangement with the County Education Committee, who employ him as boiler-man/groundsman. This particular year, it was Tommy Stubbs, an honest worker, who had turned out for West Ham in the Late Middle Ages. It was written into his contract that he was to supply an amalgam of brain and experience.

There was no village nor hamlet in our county that didn't nourish a deep and abiding hate for Barchester, whose citizens were a smug lot, believing that the world stopped beyond their last house. Only that same year, a resident canon compiling a guide book for the National Tourist Board, having gushed out 54 pp. over his Cathedral and its Environs, crammed eighteen surrounding villages into the last 4 pp., sprinkled with such venomous and belittling adjectives as 'squalid', 'unkempt', 'sluttish' and, bitterest blow, 'devoid of interest'. So at least seven local games were postponed so that players and supporters could come and yell against the Holy Boys. In fact, it should be put in the *Guinness Book of Records* that this was the only time in the History of Football when an away side had the more supporters.

We went in Mr Tate's bus, whose *raison d'être* was emptying Steeple Sinderby, Ainderby, Bag Enderby and Middle Marsh of their children into Barchester Bishop Beauchamp C. of E. Comprehensive School, where, said Mrs Fangfoss, who had been convent-educated, 'they train them to smash bus shelters, mug elderly ladies, set light to cats with paraffin and to whine in chorus that the world owed them a living'.

It had forty springless seats into which you sank so deep that I know of several passengers who caught hernias escaping from them. The fare to supporters was 50p and this included a package deal of egg and bacon at Jacks Caff on the by-pass. It was over-subscribed, and there was a lot of ill-feeling because five young women took this heaven-sent chance to escape from Sinderby and shop on a Saturday, which normally is impossible unless you have a car.

There was no nonsense about our players travelling free like some miserable village sides, who wring their fares from old-age pensioners lured to whist-drives by a bit of warmth and sociability. Alex Slingsby's precept for this – and he had one for about everything covering our activities (see Appendix in the Official History) – ruled that 'Sport is fun and Fun has to be paid for'. This derived from his hard upbringing; his dad having been a Baptist lay preacher had marked him with uncompromising rectitude. So only one man went for nothing, Corporal, and this was only because he had nothing.

I don't expect to be believed, but Barchester not Wembley was the ground that stands supreme in memory's pages for me. Two reasons. (1) To us, Barchester City was the first of the Big Boys. Last season we couldn't even have imagined playing let alone defeating them, so this was the Moment of Truth. (2) And then there was the Cathedral, a great grey wall along one touch-line. It was Norman and it was Massive and it stunned me by its groaning bulk. Now this isn't the airy-fairy our Chairman warned me of. If Dr Kossuth had been there, he would have understood. But I shall now quote Ginchy Trigger's report in the *Messenger*.

WEIGHED IN BALANCE
HOLY BOYS FOUND WANTING

Beneath Barchester's venerable pile, its ancient stones etc. . . . yet another citadel crumbled before all-conquering Sinderby Wanderers. It was the old, old story when Referee Charlie McGill from Aylesbury piped his summons to the fray. Up went the ball into City's box and every Ringer except Monkey Tonks was there a-swinging, it falling to the lot of Jack Midgely, the Bag Sinderby blacksmith, to hammer it into the net. In vain venerable City Father Stubbs rallied his shaken lads. Ten minutes later Alex Slingsby nodded in a corner from Vicar Giles Montagu.

During the interval City may still have believed themselves victims of a freak storm that had now blown itself out. But they must have known they were for the chopper when, in the first minute, Sid Swift drifted off towards the chancel end, turned like a lizard and, though doughty Tom Dutton flung himself at the ball, it was flicked from his fingers and dribbled into the net. After that, the hand moved in big print across the Wall . . . etc.

Barchester City o Steeple Sinderby Wanderers 6.

Goals – Midgely, Slingsby, Swift (2), Sledmer, Hutton.

While I was waiting in joyous mood for Tate's bus to pick me up, I strolled along to the Square by the Cathedral where on Saturdays they had a market. By then the stalls had gone and, replacing the traders, was Biddy, bold as brass, preaching her Religion to a sizeable crowd, mostly listening respectfully. They plainly had gathered to stare at the Shooting Star who had wrought such havoc that day but, to their astonishment, now found themselves fascinated by this big beautiful young woman and her doom-talk. An Englishman is partial to doom-talk and always has been, as is demonstrated by the nightmare stone carvings all over Barchester Cathedral, and misses it now that the Church doesn't go in for Religion raw, red and bleeding any more. Our countrymen appreciate confirmation that Hell yet prevails and that it is well on the cards that they are thither bound.

'Now,' Biddy was crying with immense conviction, 'anybody here who has more than two children is mankind's enemy. And some must not be allowed to perpetuate their subselves even *once*. There is, there *must* be such degenerates in your own street. Their animal passions – yes, these they may indulge, but only when they are sterilized . . .'

At this, one brave soul cried out, 'Is it God's will?'

'Don't talk to me of *that*,' cried Biddy with a new access of passion and waving a dismissive hand at the grey bulk behind her. 'A million little children poured into the gas ovens, ten million fathers crucified on barbed wire – my good man, ask *them* for an answer. God? You are your own gods . . .'

'Please ma'am, may I ask a question?' a man cried.

'Ask!' Biddy said.

'Will Mr Swift tell us if he shoots harder with his left or his right foot?'

Instead of turning this defaulter into stone, Biddy turned a long and searching truthbeam on Sid, who immediately stumbled forward.

'Friend,' he said in hoarse and earnest tones, 'trembling as we all are on the brink of Hell, how *can* you bother your head with trivial things? If the world's chemical industries are allowed to keep pouring their poisonous waste over our food, whether it be spuds in the field or fish in the sea, *your* grandson will be born without either a right *or* a left foot.'

Biddy nodded encouragingly and this plainly meant more to Sid than roaring terraces. Why, he was a second Lazarus! I was staggered. And then irritated beyond all reason – the bus drew up and they yelled for me to get in.

On the following Monday we heard that we had drawn Tetford United in the next round and, on the next Friday evening, the playing squad plus Mr Fangfoss and me met in the Bull's backroom. Because I was instructed not to take any minutes I may not be as accurate as usual. But, near enough, it went like this . . .

'So far you've done all you've been asked,' Alex said. 'But at the back of your minds, it's all a bit of a giggle. All right, you're thinking, we've beaten Barchester City and so what – that always *was* on the cards – and OK we might just do the next one as well – *but when the Big Boys come in* . . . and to those faint-hearts I'm on at, the Big Boys mean Football League Division 4 . . . Oh, so you're all looking mimm as though such horrible thoughts could never enter your heads. Right! I'll show you. You've brought your strip. All right. Boots on the table! Here's mine for a start . . .'

And out they came and, in a heap, they were a truly repulsive sight. Not only me . . . everybody saw *that*, and the merciless scrutiny that followed was not strictly necessary: the boots themselves cried out. No one spoke.

'There are two pairs match-fit,' he said. 'Sid's and mine. The rest range from awful to disgraceful – Barchester mud-pancake soles, mildewed uppers, a stink of foot-rot, worn studs, some missing, crippling nails . . . if these items of footwear reflect your approach to the Tetford game, then God help us. Joe

Gidner might as well drop their secretary a line to give them the match and we'll save our bus fares.

'From now on, Sunday morning is scrape, sponge, nail and lace check, dubbin, leather massage. Your boots are part of your feet. Lads, we must *think* football and *dream* football. All eleven of us and the reserves! If we're beaten, we must leave the pitch knowing there was nothing, *nothing*, NOTHING at all we'd left undone that we could have done. That way, I, for one, won't mind losing. And believe me, a match can hang on a worn stud, a stride lost, an instant's lapse of concentration.

'And don't think the eye of the world is on you. Outside this county we don't exist. Until November, the FA Cup is just a horrible scuffle to scoop up minnows to feed the big fishes. But, we're going through, *we're going through*, and when we're fed in, that club, whichever it is, will find us mouthful enough to choke it.'

I think he wasn't talking to us any more. Then who? Perhaps Fate! Daring it! Then he came back to earth and handed round a sheet he'd run off on the school duplicator.

Tetford United – top of the Fenland League and have been for last three seasons. Population 11,000. Chief industry Pilling's Plastics, who own football ground, pay groundsman, maintain Club HQ. They employ five ex-pros in soft jobs, let side have time off for training. The Norwich evening paper reports much grousing at waste of home FA Cup round playing a team from swede-land, claims it will put less in the Tetford kitty than a normal league game.

Well, we brooded over this to fill in the time whilst some of the slower readers struggled through it. Then Giles said, 'Well, it seems we all have our problems, Alex.' The chill went out of the air – and everybody began to laugh.

*

On Tuesday morning, the word went round the village that Percy Billison had died in the night. His unmarried sister Ethel, seeing his blinds drawn at eleven in the morning, let herself in and found him head first in his burnt-out TV.

'Well, TV was his god and it stretched forth a fiery hand and gathered him in,' Biddy commented. 'Percy was honoured above most men to have so personal a summons.'

But Mr Billison's departing was not the bad news: that came a little later in the day.

It was hard to see Miss Billison's eyes behind her thick glasses, but I always had supposed them glittering resentfully day and night. She was one of those women who had sacrificed herself to care many a long year for her aged parents. Though, when you come to think about it, this might not be the awful fate its victims make it out to be. Husbands can be tyrants and children monsters. Whereas you can care for aged parents from a chair most of the time. You don't have to turn out into the weather when the streets are slush and a streaming cold is coming on. And it also is something you can complain about and then award yourself the unspoken sympathy of your audience. You can also savour your resentment. And Miss Billison's chief resentment was Giles, because the last Vicar's wife had a private income and had given her good as new garments, whereas Biddy had typecast her as one of the undeserving poor.

So the funeral had been thoughtfully laid on for three o'clock to synchronize with the kick-off at Tetford.

'But he never set foot in the church. He didn't even attend his own mother's funeral,' cried Mrs Fangfoss passionately. 'Nor has he once forked out a penny piece towards keeping one stone on top of another. We *must* have the Vicar on the right wing, so he must tell the Billisons they'll have to cart their Percy to Barchester Crem and see him off there.' Both women had their supporters and the village divided joyfully into camps.

Do not take this too hardly. You have to understand that, in rural England, people live wrapped tight in a cocoon; only their eyes move to make sure nobody gets more than themselves. Popular education has not touched them; they communicate as their fathers did by a flick of the eyeballs, passing down grudges either improved upon or, at very least, in mint condition, from generation to generation. And of such sturdy stock were the Billisons, who now stood on their ancient Rights to have Percy dug into the holy acre fattened by many a Billison before him and at such a time most convenient to a tribal gathering.

'It's no use,' said Giles, 'I can't ask another priest to take it. After all, the Billisons are my flock. If it was summer . . . if it was a wedding, that would have been different . . .'

But Mrs Fangfoss would have none of this and swept into a massive frontal assault upon the Billison doorstep, firing a withering tirade that she, for one, wasn't going to work her fingers to the bone at bazaars and garden fetes keeping the steeple standing, just for any heathen to make a convenience of it whenever it suited him. Miss Billison's answer was brief. She declared bitterly and probably truthfully that Billisons were Sinderby freeholders before churches were thought of, when those Fawcetts (Mrs Fangfoss's maiden name) who weren't tinkers were rotting either on the gibbet or in the house-of-correction, and that when she (Mrs Fangfoss) had been in Sinderby another fifty years, only then might she consider herself a real Sinderbian. And she could pass on this glad news to her imbecile sister, Fangfoss's concubine.

She then dispatched a male Billison to Barchester to complain to the Archdeacon, who, poor man, was terribly upset. He properly recoiled from offending good money-raisers like Mrs Fangfoss but there *was* canon law and, since there was no documentary proof that the Billisons were Baptists or Methodists, they must be C. of E. by default. So he washed his hands of it and handed the business back to Mr Fangfoss, in his capacity as churchwarden. So our Chairman, putting on a mask of extreme affability, declared he wanted only to play the game with all parties, do everything straight and above board, and offered to settle the bill for the funeral and all fittings from his own pocket – cortège, flowers, funeral feast and a handsome memorial stone – so long as they had it done at the Crem. But Miss Billison scornfully refused, telling all she met in shop and street of her stand. Billisons had always been put in the church-yard and Percy must lie alongside his fathers.

This was the only time I've ever seen Mr Fangfoss's invin-cible composure rocked. 'Mr Gidner,' he said, 'Mr Gidner, I state this solemnly, hand on heart, that evil woman will plunge to Hell to feed her brother's flame.' He then pushed his face close to mine and declared, 'That man died just to spite the Wanderers, Mr Gidner.'

This manifestly was crazy. You can't pass away to order, unless it is with a shotgun in your mouth and a string looped round your big toe, and this he knew just as well as I did, and I have only reported his words as proof of his deep feelings.

'What shall we do?' I asked Alex helplessly.

'*We?*' he said. '*We* shall do different things. Ten others and myself will ready ourselves for Tetford United. *We* shall think football and dream football, and *we* shall not bother our heads about anything but football. As far as the eleven of us are con-cerned Percy Billison is still a live man, staring in a glass darkly. If you mean "What are *you* going to do?", that is your business and I don't want to hear a breath of it.'

Actually, it ended quite simply. The Vicar just said that it was his job and, of course, he would do it. And this he did and if, during the interment, his mind wandered over to Tetford, not even Miss Billison's condemnatory eye noticed it. In fact, he made so workmanlike a job of it that, from that time on, the

Billisons spoke nothing but in praise of him and, on succeeding Saturdays, their men always stood on his wing and shouted exclusively for him.

Oddly enough, this incident brought us our first mention in the national press. *The Times* Diary picked it up from our local paper and, below the title, *Sinderby's Path of Glory leads but to the Grave*, wrote a skit in poor taste on Thomas Gray's 'Elegy in a Country Churchyard' and, because there was no economic crisis on just then, the same paper printed folk letters usually crowded out by publicity-mad politicians. I quote this as typical of them:

From Brigadier Maitland-Trevers.
Sir,
    In this age when trivialities and vanities are expensively disguised by public relations experts into the Eternal Verities, it is reassuring to read of the simple parson of a sequestered vale putting away the tinsel of glory and turning aside to teach some rustic moralist to die.

And this letter moved an elderly lady living in a Torquay private hotel to send £25 to buy coal and knitting wool 'for the Poor of the Village, to be distributed as the Vicar thought fit', in recognition of his rebuke to a sports-crazed generation.

And so, leaving behind Fred Billison's Last Farewell and, this time, with two bus-loads of supporters, we went to Tetford through miles of swede-land very much like our own, and as empty as the countryside is on Saturdays. Ginchy Trigger sat chattering next to me and I found this pleasantly disturbing.

Because football was paid for by the plastics firm to keep its workers' minds off the revolution, the clubhouse fitments were very superior, beautifully clean, having chrome-plated showers, deep communal baths, toilets with locks, that also flushed, and a bar. There were also oak-framed photographs of past teams sitting with the company managing director. Alex and Sid, having seen Better Days, were indifferent to such ostentation – as were the Cascob Main colliers (from being brought up in a patriarchal society which required their women to swab them down daily). But the less sophisticated players went around *touching* things.

Then Corporal reeled in. 'Ref's out,' he said. One or two of the lads made for the door. Then, without prompting, drew back and let Alex go. 'After me, Sid,' he said.

The sun was still fairly high and we won the toss. I heard Alex say to his link-man, 'I want a couple of ballooners – the sun's in their eyes. Plumb in their area.'

Here is Ginchy's report in *The Messenger*.

TETFORD TIPPLED BY THE RINGERS

Summer suns were glowing when Ref Jim Hall blew up on Pilling's Plastics plush playground. After sixty seconds a mortar bomb fired by Harry Hardcastle, our Sinderby back, exploded on their penalty spot and before their K. Clark, dazzled by the sun, could clear, our Sid Swift, the Ringers' chief chimer, struck it past a flabbergasted keeper. Joe McGonigle, the ex-Dundee pro, urged his men to 'play it cool' but ten minutes later The Ringers gonged another. Once again Harry Hardcastle sent up a rocket, three Ringers dived in amongst the hen roost and this time it was Dickie Hutton who rang the till . . .

That will be as much of Ginchy Trigger's bizarre prose any reader can be asked to peruse. Enough to say that three more goals came before the final whistle. It wasn't a very interesting game. That early goal unsettled Tetford and they stayed at sixes and sevens till the end. The Tetford team was too weary to show any reaction except weariness, and the only show of spirit came from a small boy who yelled, 'Sinderby S***!' as he fled, and from the Pilling's Plastics groundsman, who wouldn't let us use his hot showers. Nor could the Tetford skipper make him, he replying that he was on Pilling's payroll and took his orders only from the General Manager, who anyway 'left everything to him'.

Village people relish sociability so long as it is cheap and, furthermore, because they are poorer than townspeople, eating out is a great treat for them. So we called at Jacks Caff, which was quiet, the lorries being off the roads. His tea came foaming from a copper boiler and his speciality sandwiches garnished with a secret recipe dressing were famous along the truck routes and even on Continental Autobahns, though seemingly it was no secret to local residents, who unkindly swore he rendered down anything, including humans, that strayed across his clients' death-dealing paths.

Be that as it may. Whilst eating, I had a most interesting chat with Mrs Fangfoss, who indignantly told me her romance books were never reviewed in the papers nor stocked by public librarians. 'It's because *they* say mine isn't Literature,' she said bitterly. 'But really it's because mine haven't enough Filth in for them. So *my* readers have to *buy* books. Even so, I have several albums of thank-you letters from nobility down to cotton spinners . . .'

This seemed a great shame to me and, sitting next to her sister on the next stage of our journey, I ventured to hint as much. 'But do you mind!' she sniggered. 'Our Theresa's books are all the same except for their titles. They are about a lonely spinster who goes on a foreign package tour and meets a good-looking count with black hair who is just going to take her off to his castle when she gets a telegram saying her old dad had a stroke and she must hurry off home. Whereas Life isn't like that . . .' And she gave me a painful dig with her elbow.

Her strong views surprised me, particularly as it is said she can't read. 'What does Mr Fangfoss think about Mrs Fangfoss's books?' I asked. 'Oh, Artie – he had a go but said he couldn't get into 'em,' she giggled. Then she gave me another dig – 'And he forbid me to put pen to paper. He says my bent lies in another direction and it's to stay there . . .'

I merely mention this social occasion because it put every-one in such a state of camaraderie that one man and three women volunteered for painting and decorating our LNER coach up to Pilling's Plastics standard, and two distant rela-tions of the Billisons whispered to Mrs Fangfoss that they had been on her side but wouldn't want it known.

Tuesday morning's papers informed us that we had been drawn away again – to Tampling Athletic, who, at the time, were standing third in the Southern League Premier Division. Two or three years before, they had canvassed around for votes for admission to the 4th Division of the Football League but, although Newport County had been bottom of this for the last four seasons, it was quietly put around that they must be toler-ated as a pocket of resistance against Welsh rugby. This injustice had discouraged Tampling, so they'd let quite a promising local centre-forward go to West Ham for £4,000 and, for £2,000, replaced him by Sandy McGovern, an aged Scots international fallen on hard times. This profit paid for a hand-some new directors' lounge and bar, with a shatter-proof picture-window, and to have that part of the car park nearest to it asphalted.

After Tetford, we had to catch up with our Barchester & District League games and, as it got dark about 4 o'clock, we had to play two games on the same Saturday, one at home v. Bennington British Rail and one away against Bollinger's Brewery. Although it would have been policy to have used one of these as a practice game for our best team, we feared a com-plaint from the club left to face our Second XI might result in us being fined. So we split our forces and Alex captained one game and Giles Montagu the other. Sid Swift was rested; that is to say he'd been taken off to Cambridge by Biddy for a one-day Conference of Minority Religions, and everybody approved of this as it had been noted how strongly these evangelical toppings-up came out in his football.

The home game was against the railwaymen. They brought a large crowd with them and we took £2.35 at the gate. There was some grumbling that Sid Swift and Alex weren't playing but, on the whole, they were pleased to win 1–0 and take the two points home, boasting they'd beaten Tetford's conquerors. But, over at Turley, it was a different matter altogether. This is Ginchy Trigger's report in *The Messenger*.

FROTHBLOWERS DRAIN DEFEAT TO DREGS

From the whistle till Referee O'Grady mercifully called Time the Brewery Boys were plugged into their Areas as tight as a barrel's bung. Despite several casualties – two were carried off and one retired without permission and wouldn't come back – they took their medicine like men.

During the closing moments we were astonished to see that George Adams, the only one of Bollinger's eleven goalies permitted to use his hands, had moved across and joined Monkey Tonks in the Sinderby goal. It was later revealed he had collided with an upright and was suffering from a loss of memory. George is now 100% again. But 2 goalies in one goal! Is this a record?

Bollinger's Brewery Athletic 0
Steeple Sinderby Wanderers 7

MINUTES OF MEETING HELD DEC. 1ST IN THE BLACK BULL.

Present. Chairman, Mr Fangfoss. Messrs. Slingsby, Montagu, Ormskirk and Hon. Sec.

Apologies. Mr J. Bleasby, who had sent word he had to chaffeur his employer, Sir Edward Furlong, to a banquet.

The Secretary read the minutes of the last meeting & there were no matters arising.

Giving his report, the Captain, Mr Slingsby, itemized recent playing results and expressed qualified satisfaction with his side's record. He announced that our team would play Tampling Athletic of the Southern League in the next qualifying round of the FA Cup.

At the Chairman's wish playing members were now admitted to the meeting for a discussion of Kossuth Postulation 6 –

A *Home* team's only advantage is feeling *at home*.
Visiting sides should therefore feel *at home* also.

Mr Slingsby then invited questions and Mr Swift requested information on Tampling's gates.

Mr Slingsby replied that numbers ranged from 400 in cold, wet weather when the side was having a bad spell, to 3,000 for cup-ties under floodlight on warm evenings, following a periodic exhortation from the *Tampling Sentinel* for more public spirit.

Our Chairman asked for information about his *vis-à-vis*, the Tampling Chairman. Mr Slingsby replied that he was a prominent property speculator and town councillor who had the knack of guessing where new housing development will be. There also were other prestigious local figures on the Board, mostly in it for Puff and for the allocation of Wembley tickets.

Our Chairman followed with a supplementary question which I quote verbatim – 'Does the Big Feller keep 'em going out of his own pocket?'

Mr Slingsby replied that he was sorry if his early statement might have given the impression that this must be so. But it was not so, the club's finances being largely provided by the Supporters' Club, who ran a football pool, the admin complexities of which, in recent years, had put two treasurers in jail and another in mental hospital. The Supporters' Club had no representation on the Board but was invited to the Annual General Meeting. The present Chairman of the Supporters' Club was the Football Club's Chairman's chief clerk.

Mr Fangfoss then asked, 'What is the Southern League?'

Requesting that his remarks would not be reported to the Press, Mr Slingsby said this League had been described by some as the Waiting Room for Div. 4 of the Football League and by others as a hovering flock of vultures willing some poor straggler to fall. But no one disputed that it was a drab, boring, irritating league where nobody even remembered last season's champion. Most of the performers would never move on to anything better, and sides were sprinkled with players on their way down from better days, with maybe a couple of seasons left. After the thunder of the Kop, the Southern League was a bitter pill to swallow but it helped pay the butcher . . .

'And your last word is?' asked Mr Fangfoss.

Mr Slingsby answered that Tampling could be, but would not expect to be, beaten. He expressed a hope for a quick goal, or better still, a couple, whilst Tampling were still showing their crowd the difference between professionals and amateurs.

Our Chairman, deviating from custom, closed the Meeting by opening his Bible at random and reading us a Message. This being Matt. 24 v. 28. 'Wheresoe'er the carcase is, there shall the eagles be gathered.'

After reflecting on this Great Truth the Meeting adjourned.

When this whole business was over – the Cup Final I mean – it dawned on many of us that we were no longer the same people we'd been a year earlier. Without realizing it, we'd raised our game.

Three months earlier it would have been beyond belief that I might improve on the Doctor himself. But that's what I did – I expanded Postulation 6, the one which drew attention to the advantages enjoyed by a home side. The Doctor had suggested that an away side should '*think itself at home*'. It was during one of Giles's sermons, when I did most of my serious thinking, that it came to me – 'an away side should *think* itself at home AND THEN MAKE THE HOME SIDE FEEL LESS AT HOME'.

Reluctantly, I must now introduce Maisie Twemlow into the picture. Maisie was the last living fan of John Lennon, and wore big round steel-rimmed glasses to prove it. She also had long dank hair, a flat chest and thick ankles. Nor had she any redeeming spiritual or intellectual compensation, any tenderness or sparkle. All she had was Force and the knack of organizing kindred spirits and injecting Force into them also.

Overall, I can best describe her as the re-incarnation of some ancient Greek Fury. And her band looked astonishingly like her. In between bouts of hysteria, they sat around and knitted away like madwomen and, as madness is well known to infect others, their mothers and aunts began knitting madly as well. On Saturdays they gathered in sagging knitted buttercup coats, their heads tied on with buttercup scarves. Then, armed with handbells, they ran and rang and wailed. Many was a time that season, I witnessed an immense crowd prick its ears like Neanderthal Man smelling Danger. There had been no sound like it on English football grounds ever before, nor, I have heard, even in the Argentine. Nevertheless, to make my theory work of making home sides feel less at home, I recruited and encouraged these monsters, but let Mr Fangfoss and Alex suppose that their conduct was quite spontaneous.

So we went to Tampling and as our four buses drew into the town's central car park, Maisie and her Furies shot out, wailing and jangling down the middle of High Street, bringing trade and traffic to a halt, causing babies to cry and old-age

pensioners to clutch their handbags and, significantly, casting
the vague shadow of a doubt across the minds of football supporters thronging to our sacrifice. It is true, these reasoned,
that this *is* our loved Tampling because we have just paid our
rate-demands. 'It *is* our town.' But, after more wailing and jangling, they thought, 'Is it?'

To his credit, their Chairman came to our dressing room.
'Well, lads,' he said, 'you've been having a good run for your
money. We're taking you seriously (large, glad smile) and I've
had the local rag drumming you up, so we'll have a good gate,
which I expect you'll find a change from two small boys, the
debt collector and one old horse, eh? And there's good old Sid!
Back in harness, eh, Sid? One last fling before you hang the
boots and saddle in the bicycle shed, eh?'

Sid looked blankly at him as though he'd been making his
speech in a foreign language. And when he'd gone he said
sourly, 'I wonder if we'll have a visit from Moneybags after
we've taken the hide offen 'em, and, if he comes, what'll he say?'

Their opening moves showed class and were a real treat.
They moved the ball effortlessly from man to man: more like
chess than football. Not one of our side touched the ball for
two or three minutes and the crowd loved it. 'Come on, you
Blue 'Uns!' they yelled happily. 'Come on, Tampling!'

Mostly, they were very respectable men, muffled against the
winter day in home-knitted cardigans with large leather buttons; a phlegmatic, shuffling, stamping lot, grey men who had
handed over 20p to cram close to grey men, huddling under a
grey sky in a grey landscape on their grey way to the town
cemetery. Here, lost in the throng, they had bought another
identity for ninety minutes. They bellowed disbelief at incom-
petence, cried scornfully to the grey heavens in godlike despair,
clamoured angrily for revenge. For 20p they did all this and
were not called to account.

'Come on, you Blue 'Uns! Give these big-headed buggers some stick! Kick 'em off their stocking tops!' the mild-looking man next to me yelled. 'Them and their fancy buttercup bitches!' He heard himself and stopped; then looked round furtively to make sure that no one from his street had heard him. He began to cough. And he had a graveyard cough: this was his last season.

And responding to their crowd's delight, Tampling had us retreating deep into our half. But did they notice in what good order we fell back, man marking man, no player committed beyond recovery? And Alex Slingsby, with all the time in this world, sweeping up behind them? It was football at its classic best, both sides playing with academic confidence, because both sides knew they were going to win. Pure ballet!

And then . . .

And then the dream was shattered. A vast ungainly clearance by Frank Maidstone and the nine Sinderby men pouring through the ragged gaps, cry havoc and let loose the dogs of war! No nonsense, just battering down the middle of the field and half the Tampling side only comprehending the play had gone into reverse when they saw their keeper trundling the ball from their net. It was brutal.

Then it was ding-dong until half-time and, afterwards, as shock wore off and anxiety hadn't been turned on, Tampling slowed and slackened. And thus it befell that Twiggy Sledmer chasing up his wing like a hare and, finding the Tampling defence formed up to ward him off, drove the ball from touch-line to touch-line, where Giles scooped it up, let their backs change direction towards him and then aimed at the cubic foot of air into which Sid Swift's head rose to flick it into the top left-hand corner of the net. It was one of those goals magic in their effortlessness, the pattern plain to even the simplest mind, a goal to stir the most partisan supporter to joy, win or lose.

And the Tampling crowd yelled and stamped. Then relapsed into embarrassed silence. Two down, fifteen minutes to go and anxiety becomes panic. And thus it was that R. W. Hutton scored a third a minute before time.

Their Chairman didn't visit us again but I saw him (eyes bulging) hissing at his manager. 'Poor sod,' said Sid, 'he'll be studying the Situations Vacant in Monday's paper . . .'

And their *Evening Comet*, which had just been taken over by a London-based Group and so could speak without fear or favour of a local Chairman of Directors, celebrated its freedom thus:

The Blue 'Uns downslid to a new low on Saturday, being kicked unceremoniously out of the FA Cup by a team of Saturday afternoon footballers that didn't cost a ha'penny between them. To apply for promotion to the 4th Division status for at least ten years (when Saturday mercifully might be forgotten) would be a farce. The best thing the directors can do is crawl off to Sinderby, buy its team and pick them en bloc as from next week.

Strangely enough the directors swallowed this bitter pill, because we received a letter mentioning they'd sacked their manager and asking how much our 'board' was asking for the transfer of Sid Swift, Giles, Twiggy and Alex Slingsby. 'And,' as Alex said, 'they didn't give Monkey a chance to see what he could do or they'd have wanted him as well.' Naturally, we refused and then sent their late Manager a letter of sympathy and, at Sid's request, a cheque for £10.

And now we were out of the jungle and face to face with the Football League, which rose like an unclimbable cliff from Newport Country to Carlisle.

So the First Round Proper now was upon us and into the hat tumbled the survivors of the rough and tumble preliminary rounds of

Free for All, battered and weary from too much football and staring wildly around like half-drowned men cast up from the sea, amazed to find themselves still breathing though not likely to live. And of these 30, the majority were semi-professional sides from the Southern, Northern Premier and Birmingham & District Leagues, who year after year vainly sought entrance to Div. IV and, just as regularly, had its door slammed in their faces, their stigma being lack of population not prowess.

But, among these, were three or four upstarts from utter obscurity, clubs that had never before seen their names in print outside such weekly papers as served the Barkston Ash League, the Macclesfield & Mid-Cheshire Combination and so forth. They surfaced naked and ashamed – Sandbach Ramblers, Three Sisters Colliery Welfare, Bodmin Borough, the Royal Ouse-side Cooperative Wholesale Society Sports and Social Fellowship. And us – Steeple Sinderby Wanderers!

Now all that had been going on in Sinderby was pretty exciting to me and, I'd like to suppose now, to you. Indeed, there's no denying that it *was* exciting but, unfortunately, since the Media didn't direct attention to it, it has only become accepted as exciting now that it's over and done with. At the time, it has to be said that, outside our county, the Wanderers' feats raised neither pip nor squeak. News, for the most part, is manufactured and, by inference, anything not packaged by TV and the papers is not merchandise. Mind you, in the light of what happened later, I must say that if there is one thing worse than being ignored by the Media, it is being taken up by it.

So when the draw was announced, imagine hard-pressed Sports Editors finding this foreign name, Sinderby, on the FA's press release. Yeovil, they knew, Wigan Athletic, Dulwich Hamlet, Bishop Auckland and Norton Woodseats, they knew. Every odd year or so, all these glimmered faintly before being snuffed out. But Steeple Sinderby . . . ?

'Only a handful of Hartlepool supporters will bother to travel to the little Welsh market town . . .'

Mirror.

'Steeple, the tiny Yorkshire colliery village, is host to Hartlepool . . .'

Telegraph.

'Old Grandfer Fangfoss, trainer of the villagers, squeezed a chuckle from his toothless jaws as he sat over a noggin beside his cottage door. "Oi sez our lads'll win 'em, mi jolleys," he piped, running a horny hand over his luscious sixteen year old bride's bouncy boobies . . .'

Sun.

'Steeple Sinderby Wands v. Hartlepool.'

The Times.

From this point on, I shall not say a great deal about the actual playing preparations, being almost totally engrossed in seeing to other details. Top clubs keep a big staff – Secretary, Treasurer, Groundsman, Publicity Manager, right down to the chaps to de-litter the stands and fiddle the turnstiles. Well, at Sinderby, all these jobs were mine and I still had to find time to pay my way by composing greetings card verses.

In these trying times, my prop, pillar and support was our Chairman. This great man has never been recognized for what he was – an administrative Napoleon. He knew nothing about football and had never undergone a Managerial Efficiency Course. Later, when asked to explain himself by an Organiza-tion & Methods Expert, he answered simply, 'It is because I am not an Expert. Experts invent themselves. Whereas I was born *with my mind made up'*.

So when I went to him with my problem of dealing with the crowd expected for the Hartlepool game, he at once advanced

£400 for defence works, saying he would recoup this in part by making two large meadows at the entrance of the village into temporary car-parks. And without consulting them, he also proffered Mrs Fangfoss and her sister to run a tea bar in the further field, so that everybody didn't try to leave together on the one road out of the village.

By Wednesday night two of his men, released from beet loading, had fortified Parson's Plow with a six-band barbed-wire fence on the inside of the thorn hedge, and a second entanglement inside that. He had the field gate taken off its hinges and replaced by a high fence of one-inch planks, leaving two gaps wide enough to let in one man at a time sideways. Meanwhile, his friend Mr Burgoyne, the Barchester builder, knocked up two tiers of planks right round the playing area making three levels – the turf, one step up and one step up again, but all at the same admission price. We reckoned we could have 600 standing each side and 300 at each end.

Alex's father-in-law, Mr Croser, agreed to take the money at one slit and Mr Issitt, the district rate-collector (£1 honorarium), the other. I was released from any pre-arranged jobs to deal with any unforeseen occurrences and, to this end, fixed up a system of runners provided by Maisie Twemlow.

As Mr Fangfoss allowed no crime in Sinderby, we didn't have a constable, but he asked Sgt Kettlewell from the police post at Cascob Colliery to check our arrangements. The Sergeant's information network, which local publicans provided in return for elastic closing hours, estimated there would be enough local bodies alone to fill our 1,800 spaces, and that some disturbance could be expected from Hartlepool coach-loads arriving too late to get in. But he felt his presence inside the ground and PC Codd's outside would be enough to overawe them.

'All right,' Mr Fangfoss said. 'I'll get the Electric to rig up loudspeakers in that old orchard of mine down by the brook, and them that can't get into the Plow can stand under the trees and listen. And you fix up somebody to tell 'em over the loud-speakers who's winning.'

So I asked Ginchy Trigger and she agreed to do a commentary at no charge, saying it would be good practice for when she got on BBC *Sportsnight*.

Having real professional footballers come to Sinderby was terribly exciting. Even Hartlepool, hanging half out of the floor of the 4th Division. They stayed the night at the George in Barchester, and Twemlow's spies soon were sending encouraging intelligence bulletins. Four of their team had been in or behind the back-room of Jacks Caff till one in the morning and the rest, by arrangement with Sgt Kettlewell had stayed boozing in the Fleece. But when eventually I did set eyes on them, what actually impressed me was their clobber – they truly were sharp dressers – scarcely a one that didn't have a hundred and fifty pounds' worth hung about him. But the brightness was all in their raiment, most of them having prehistory brows. And Sid, like a comet lost for a thousand years in outer space now reappearing in familiar skies, cast a cold eye over them and made a brief godlike judgment – 'They're jam rabble, dirty swine what'll turn vicious when we down 'em.' And when I suggested that, if this was so, they must be highly suitable material for Biddy and him to work on, he took a second look. 'No use,' he said. 'Too far gone.'

Saturday was a crisp, clear autumn day, firm and dry, a day so perfect for watching football that queues leapt in length and, a half-hour before kick-off, were a quarter-mile long at each slit in the fence. So, although the two Twemlowites who had endured so much for us behind Jacks Caff looked pretty rough, I hardened my heart and made them roam two sides of the pitch apiece and report back when the three levels were almost full. When they confirmed this, I sent word to Mr Croser to bar the entrances. There was some roaring from those within sight of the tickets, but local folks broke off and ran round into the next fields because, having first-hand knowledge of how inefficient arrangements usually were at rural garden fetes and so on, they were sure there would be a gap left somewhere. They soon trailed despondently back. I think it was the narrow pit between the outer and inner barbed-wire fences that put the wind up them.

Meanwhile, I had set a rumour going that the Overflow Orchard was filling up, and this drained off part of the mob. But even so, a multitude still drifted restlessly outside Parson's Plow and these were the ones that gave me concern, because they would be most easily inflamed by the shouting from the battlefield itself.

Seated at my command post, like the outcasts in the Orchard, my only link with the actual game was Ginchy Trigger's commentary. And she seemingly watched with her mouth wide open, only remembering to speak when nothing was going on.

'The Hartlepool team is emerging. They are wearing red shirts, white shorts, white stockings with red bands round their tops. They have brought two new balls and are kicking them very expertly. And here are the Ringers in their familiar all-gold strip, though some say it's more the colour of buttercups. They have only brought one ball and it's an old one. We have another but we are keeping that for the game itself . . .

'Here comes the ref Mr Hicks is from Accrington, which is Yorkshire. He is examining the nets for holes – as if there'd be any – and now he has called up the captains to make them shake hands. Alex Slingsby has won it, by that I mean he has won the toss and has put Hartlepool in to face the sun . . .'

Then there were almighty shouts from first one end and then the other and, plainly, both sides were near getting a goal. But nothing was vouchsafed from Ginchy: the loudspeakers in the trees stayed silent. So I got as close to where I believed her to be and yelled, 'Tell them what's going on. The folks in the orchard! Tell them quick or I'll have them bursting in at the fence.' And she must have heard me.

'The Hartlepool left wing keeps ballooning the ball over everybody's head and their right wing doesn't get it high enough. I think they can't get used to the side slope . . . Now they're losing their tempers with one another and there's Sid Swift he's going to the left wing no he isn't he's running to the right wing he's slipped it to our parson on the way and he's charged one of them over and flashed it back to where Sid's gone which is in the middle . . . I'm sorry I missed the next bit because a great lout knocked me off my plank with two others BUT IT'S IN, IT'S IN and they say Sid did it. And that makes two for Us.'

Soon after half-time one of the Maisie Twemlow girls reported that a fight had broken out behind the Hartlepool goal where a wad of Teessiders had been baiting the local supporters – first banteringly but, after the second goal, turning ugly, and sinking to 'turnip-heads', 'swede-bashers', 'clod-hoppers' and, from one who must have passed the eleven-plus, 'peasants'. All of which our Sinderby men bore with sangfroid, each persuading himself that these insults were directed at some other person. Naturally this did nothing to assuage the anger of the visitors, who, finding jeers to no avail, began shoving, elbowing and treading around until, eventually, one youth plucked off the trilby hat of Mr Greenslade, Lord Spooner's gamekeeper, this hat having significance for him because he'd been married in it. This was tossed on to the pitch and its owner bade to 'ga on doon and fetch it, goo' dog!' Whereupon Mr Greenslade (who was a well-known believer in Self-help, and dead against the unions, women's rights, extra-marital sex and the black nations) struck his persecutor a mighty back-hander which witnesses wonderingly declared knocked him through the two rear ranks, carrying three others with him to the greensward . . . from which they rose and, in true English fashion, uncomplainingly resumed their places as though nothing out of the way had happened. Except the Hartlepool lout, who lay slobbering as the blood dribbled between his fingers.

And there he stayed till two strong girls dragged him to the tent, where Mrs Trencher, the District Nurse, told him not to be so big a booby and held his head down by the hair whilst inserting her sovereign remedy, a large house-key, down his spine.

Back to Ginchy Trigger,

'One of their players has lost his temper after a charge and he has knocked down the Vicar. He did it with his fist. And Alex Slingsby has made all ours sit down like little Indians and how sensible of him. Mr Hicks is sending the puncher off. It just looks to me as if these big league sides can't bear to be beaten and they're going to be beaten because we're better than they are.

'They've just carried Giles off and Jack Crummock's gone off as well but I can't tell what's happened to him. Kicked I expect. We've brought back both our wingers. We've brought back Sid as well, all our side is back round Monkey Tonks and it's like a battlefield, bodies everywhere the ball's cannoning off everybody left right and centre if it isn't one of us it's one of them and three spectators behind our goal have been knocked down as well. And there's another fight there again and one of them has been told to go off and he won't. Now he's going. Just because we're winning. And Frank Maidstone's down as well and he's rolling over. They're all around Monkey Tonks and he's trying to push them away as he can't see. And everybody's running into one another and the ball's knocked two of theirs down. HE'S

RUNNING! BILLY SLEDMER'S RUNNING! There's nobody in front of him but their goalie and he's coming out crouching. HE'S SCORED! We've got THREE. THEY CAN'T WIN US NOW! I am going to interrupt this commentary to go and see to our Vicar.'

This third goal must have brought on a suicidal mood of despair amongst the Hartlepool crowd outside the ground. They genuinely may have supposed that their players were being set upon by the natives and, rallied by a middle-aged man in a flat cap, they drove at the fence, which stood fast, and, when some of them tried to climb over, they were either dragged back by Constable Codd or had their fingers rapped with broom sticks by Mr Croser, who had cleverly foreseen such a crisis. And these fell back on their fellows, uttering loud cries of pain and indignation that anyone should dare to use them thus lawlessly.

Foiled in this assault, they wheeled in good order, burst into the next field and, having first forced a gap in the hawthorn hedge, threw their top-coats to mask the barbs on the outer fence and hoisted a spearhead of three into the trap between the two entanglements. But, instead of heeding the cries of their advance party for more coats to help breach the inner fence, an undisciplined support column also burst across, forcing the first lot against the naked hooks so that they began to scream with pain and terror.

No one able to see the game took slightest heed of this minor drama so Maisie Twemlow, myself and two of her girls began tearing them clear as they really were in a most awful mess and, but for the desperate crisis, I could have pitied them. Then Catastrophe! The second fence sagged and gave way and, trampling their fallen comrades into the barbed wire, a second wave swept over. God, it was like pictures of the Western Front, and worse – grown men weeping. The barbs had torn gaping rents in their trousers and jackets. I saw one with a sleeve missing and another with his trousers ripped from crutch to turn-up. But those frenzied few that had come through unscathed threw themselves at the backs of the walls of spectators and fighting broke out all down the line.

This was the most critical incident of the day and could have had grave consequences because, if they'd broken through on to the pitch, they might well have caused the game to be abandoned, our ground to have been closed by the FA and the replay fixed somewhere else. Mercifully, at this exciting state of the game, the spectators were just as determined as their assailants and the displaced persons fought back the interlopers, so, though there were about eight Wild West saloon brawls, they were on so short a front that no one elsewhere even guessed what was going on behind. Then the whistle went.

That there was no further bloodshed was due to a circumstance even Dr Kossuth couldn't have thought up. I have already mentioned Mr Greenslade, the gamekeeper, but not that he always carried his double-bore shotgun in a wrap-over interior pocket his wife had cleverly sewn into one of Lord Spooner's cast-off Burberrys. And now, in a transport of joy at his parish's victory in what, in his simple way, he regarded as a battle rather than an athletic contest, he drew forth this firearm and fired twice into the air. On the instant, a profound hush fell on the concourse both in and out of the ground, many northerners momentarily supposing that they were now about to be put to the sword. Then each withdrew into grey anonymity and silently stole away, carefully leaving a clearing around Mr Greenslade, who, come to himself, blushed and guiltily folded his weapon back inside his coat.

His wife stopped him from attending further games.

On the following Monday afternoon I found that I couldn't give my mind to composing verses for Mother's Day (hard enough at the best of times because of the trouble I had with my own mother), so I made the best of a bad job and joined Sid Swift in his brush cupboard and we listened to the 4th Round Draw on Radio One. And it was Leeds United.

This Leeds, of course, was not a nonpareil like the Revie-managed sides of the late 60s and early 70s, and were stirring around in the lower half of the 1st Division, usually winning at home and losing away. A club's success follows a trough and wave pattern. Imaginative energy takes a club up, sloppy sentiment brings it down. You keep a player for auld lang syne, you don't vote out a Chairman of Directors slipping gently into senility – and you're on the slippery slope. The English character being what it is, only near-collapse can get things changed. Remember Aston Villa! For that matter, remember Dunkirk!

Alex and Sid stood down in the next Saturday league match and went down to Leeds's away match at Millwall to spy out the land. Alex made his report at the Monday night meeting.

'Good solid side, orthodox, still using the Alf Ramsey puppet moves. Can be prised open on your side of the can, Tinker – their backs, Coggins and Harvey, wade too far out so, at times, they have four wings. Coggins has chalked up three goals and Harvey a couple, and it's gone to their collective head. True, they're both fast, very fast for their size. Always seem to get back when they're needed. You'll be getting the ball well behind them, Tinker, and *you'll* be facing the right way. But they're not stupid, one bad scare is all the warning they'll need. So, when that ball comes, make it stick *first* time, because it'll be the *only* time. Got anything to add, Sid?'

'Baxendale,' said Sid. 'He's a clogger. Vicious nasty devil. Always was. Watch him.'

We picked the side that beat Hartlepool. The coach was to set off at 11 o'clock but, well before then, the postman on his rounds had asked Alex, more in fun than anything else, what sort of club it was that let one of its players crawl in at one on a cup-tie morning. He didn't mention any names but he lived in Gun Passage, two doors up from Jack Midgely ('Jolly Jack' as he liked to be known). Alex deliberated on this over his hard-boiled egg, the only pre-game sustenance he took. Then he went off to the Passage.

Mrs Midgely opened the door and loyally tried to stall him by suggesting that Jack came along after he'd shaved. 'I'll wait,' said Alex and, after much coming and going, downstairs, looking less than jolly, Jack traipsed in. 'There's no need to ask you: I can smell you,' said Alex. 'You won't be playing, Jack,' and left the house.

At half past nine, Giles Montagu came round and said Jack had been round to ask him to intercede. 'Wasn't dropping him on the day of the game rather rough? There's his pride. Can't we let him off with a warning?'

'He knows what we agreed on,' Alex said. 'Winning this game means more to the ten of us than saving one face. No beer-swiller can keep up the pace we've set ourselves. He'd spew up on the touch-line when the heat was on. Once discipline cracks we might as well put our coats on and go home. Young Hen Wimslow's been training hard with us like the good sport he is, on the off-chance, and he's as much to offer as Jack. Sorry, Giles, I never was a big believer in "If you do this just once more . . ."'

'Well,' the Vicar said, gazing at the ceiling, 'if anyone hasn't got the Message yet . . .'

So that was the end of Jolly Jack. He took umbrage and didn't come on the coach nor turn up for practice the following week. He wasn't picked again.

I'd never been up north before. It began at Sheffield and went on over the foothills of coal spoil through Rotherham, Barnsley,

Wombwell, Swinton, Featherstone, Normanton, and the awful wilderness skirting Leeds. Not so much black as blighted. The natives seemed to have lost heart and just let their litter lie . . . brick-strewn wasteland, drainage lakes choked with collapsed pit machinery and car bodies, the edge of one town lost in the next. Astonishingly, it was inhabited.

Despite our defeat of Hartlepool, the big clubs hadn't begun to take us seriously yet and, at home at Elland Road, the United foresaw at best a win of 3, 4 or 5–0 and, at worst, a farcical massacre of 10 or 11 that would make them look almost as daft as us.

In the event, once the battle was joined, Leeds almost fell for it just like every side from Barchester City onwards. Immediately the whistle went, Jack Crummock fired up the ball and for a few moments it wobbled up and down and around their penalty area amid scenes of gathering panic. In went the fatal shot, this time from young Hen Wimslow, but tragically it only rattled against the crossbar with an almighty thump. Their crowd breathed again.

What followed reminded me as much as anything of the board-clearing that starts a kid's game of draughts. Willie Craddock went down, rolling in unprofessional agony, and was borne away and seen no more. And five minutes later, in a pile-up in midfield, Fred Ormskirk, clutching a thigh and writhing, limped off to the left wing to convalesce, Billy Sledmer moving inside and Frank Maidstone going back.

It was plain who was next for the chopper – the Shooting Star; and, guessing this, the crowd drew a deep breath when, with two Leeds men, he rose to a cross. Pure hallucination of course, but they seemed to hang in the air, suspended in a terrifying slow motion. Then, almost as though the camera was speeded up, they dropped in a heap. Two got up and, at half-time, it was passed around the terraces that Clogger Baxendale had been carted off to the Infirmary with a dislocated jaw and the loudspeakers described him as being 'very poorly'. From that minute, the Stands took Sinderby seriously; the deadly professionalism of this dispensation of justice impressed them.

Ten minutes left and still no score. Leeds threw everything into a massive assault on our goal: there must have been twenty players milling around the area. Then Alex Slingsby collared the ball and, moving rapidly towards his own corner flag, see-sawed half their side out towards him. His next move was an academic question. (a) Would he concede a breathing-space corner? (b) Waste time by belting it deep into the stands? Neither! (c) He swivelled and lashed out in one movement and the stupefied crowd, twisting its collective neck, gaped as this torpedo skidded through the mob and on to twenty yards beyond Billy Sledmer, tearing at greyhound pace into the empty Leeds half.

When the hearts of Coggins and Harvey, the Leeds backs, restarted, they turned in pursuit. As for their goalman, ap Jenkyns, even in some Celtic nightmare no more sickening sight can have been revealed to him. He advanced. He halted. He advanced again. He despairingly flung himself at a ball flicked deftly from his fingers. Then he wisely hid his head as Coggins and Harvey thundered over him like pantomime heavies.

But no ball can have been more ushered into the back of the net than that one, and Billy even had time to step aside courteously to welcome C. & H.

There was stunned silence. Then wave after wave of cheering. And that was that.

FROM THE YORKSHIRE EVENING POST

. . . Black Prince sadly reports that, in his humble opinion, this master counter-stroke was plotted some years ago by William the Conqueror playing away at Hastings and urges the Leeds side to sign up at night school this coming spring. And now, by popular demand of our readers, I shall be reporting all future cup-ties of this astonishing amateur side. But take heed; when I say 'amateur' don't mistake me – I mean 'very professional, very unpaid'.

We came back down the A1 in great form, laughing and singing, even though Alex wouldn't let the buses stop at the pubs. And when we reached the village at ten o'clock, Ginchy Trigger put her arm in mine and, almost without realizing it, I was sitting on her mac up on Parson's Plow near a hedge. At least started off sitting. It was very enjoyable whilst it lasted. But afterwards, as always happens with me, I felt sad.

From this time on, no opponent took us anything else but very seriously and when we were drawn at home in the next round against Manchester, the sports chat was not 'By how many goals Manchester will win?' but 'Will they win?' We *were* playing at home.

ABSTRACT FROM MINUTES OF COMMITTEE MEETING HELD FEB. 6TH

At this point our Chairman asked why the Pools, by giving only one point for a home win, implied that the away side was more likely to lose. 'What are these advantages of playing at home?' he asked.

Replying, Mr Slingsby said that the home side had the feel of its own ground and listed natural topographical deviations such as bare patches, pogs, barely discernible dips and rises. He also asserted that, contrary to likelihood, sophisticated performers could sense air currents, wind swirl and suck.

But the chiefest asset, he stated, was its own crowd's noise, which subconsciously suggested to a visiting side that it would cause great emotional distress locally if it won. In closing, he had the opinion that threatening crowd noise such as emitted at Newcastle and Millwall actually induced fear amongst players far from home.

Our Chairman thereupon submitted a letter from the Chief Constable of the County.

For the attention, Chairman, Steeple Sinderby Parish Council.
Sir,

It has been brought to my attention that an association football game involving your parish and the City of Manchester will have as its venue a meadow in Steeple Sinderby on Saturday, February 14th at 2.30 p.m. I am advised by my staff that there will be an unprecedented egress into this area and in consequence vehicular units in excess of our route feasibility criteria will seek admission to my local authority's arterial traffic flow, generating unprecedented congestion to transpire.

I therefore urge you to make immediate application to the appropriate authority for this event to be diverted to Manchester or to some similar conurbation where appropriate traffic control facilities exist. It will be in order for you to quote this communication in support of such an application.

Mr Fangfoss then asked for guidance on whether Authority could enforce this, and Mr Slingsby replied that he knew of no precedent to support such manifest injustice. He further added that *any* cup-tie attracted people towards itself.

After some discussion the Meeting referred back to Dr Kossuth's Postulation Three, Section B:

Select terrain disadvantageous to passage of accurate high balls. Recommend re-siting Sinderby pitch to one as dissimilar to anything a professional footballer can have played over since he left his school playground.

Our Chairman stated that this was all he needed to make up our minds and recommended to the Secretary that he answer the letter using standard procedure as laid down by the Civil Service and Nationalized Industries. This being, after the lapse of one clear week, to acknowledge receipt of the letter and to say that its consideration would be placed on the next agenda of the appropriate committee, carefully omitting the date of the proposed meeting, which need not take place.

The Secretary was then advised to do nothing until further enquiry from the Chief Constable. He should then answer that plans were now so far advanced that, to alter them, would cause severe dislocation, not specifying what form this would take. He should then thank the Chief Constable for his well-known sympathetic attitude towards rural communities and that this would be brought to the notice of our local country-councillor.

Ah, how this once great land pants for a leader of the calibre of our Chairman, Mr Fangfoss! Then once again, as in the days of yore (to quote yet another poet), 'the meteor flag of England shall yet terrific burn'.

Obviously, we made it an all-ticket game, but Mr Fangfoss decided that it would be immoral to raise the charge for admission from the 5p with which we'd begun the season. We sent off an allocation of 500 tickets to Manchester, where the few that reached the Black Market sold for £50 and more. Locally, we announced allocation priority as follows –

One ticket per person would be allowed

Any supporter who had travelled to support us at Barchester

     "   "   "   "   "   "   "   " at Tetford

     "   "   "   "   "   "   "   " at Leeds

One ticket to Any blood relation down to 'cousin' of any player or committee member

     "   "   " Any other person able to show identification that he/she lived in any parish supplying one or more player to the side

and making personal application at the school between 9 and 5 on Saturday, when Mr Croser would be present.

There was no need to go further than that; all our tickets were sold before the last category was reached, bringing us in £60.

I then had this notice run off on the school duplicator and boys pushed it through every letter box in the parish.

NOTICE

All claims for damage occasioned by football crowds will be met in full. A sub-committee will inspect any such damage and will agree a list of repairs with the aggrieved party.

And so we made our preparations, checking each detail in the light of what we'd learnt from the Hartlepool game, massively strengthening our barbed-wire entanglements, rigging up a paddock as well as the orchard with loudspeakers, urging Ginchy Trigger to be less inflammatory in her commentary and to cut out cries of joy or horror unless she explained them, and padlocking the gate of Mr Stapleton's beet field to prevent other parking-charge dodgers joining the several Hartlepool cars and one coach sunk axle deep in the mire, which would have to await spring and a long dry spell for a deliverance.

As it turned out, many hundreds and perhaps thousands of Lancashire supporters, obeying some lemming-like impulse and ignoring the many announcements in the *Guardian* and *Evening News* that there were no tickets, streamed helplessly south. By mid-day the Chief Constable was proved a true prophet; all the county's roads were choc-a-bloc and only pedestrians could move in Barchester. Meanwhile, Mr Fangfoss's men filled meadow after meadow with cars, even his furthest, which was more than a mile from the village. The orchard filled up like a pop festival and then overflowed into the paddock. They were very orderly – and really, it was quite touching: they just looked up at the silent loudspeakers, as though supplicating some sign of favour from heaven. I have to admit that I was somewhat stirred by this unfaltering blind loyalty – contradicting, as it did, the moralists who declare that the modern Englishman cares for nothing except his own back and belly.

By mid-day the Parish was crammed with human beings, yet we were receiving incredulous reports from surrounding villages of a mountainous wave of traffic creeping forward inexorably at us.

Mr Fangfoss and I went into crisis conference and agreed that the village would soon burst apart in an eruption of violence. So we turned to Maisie Twemlow, who, immediately taking it in, said to leave everything to her and ask no questions. Then she sent four of her outriders by secret paths over field and ditch to emerge at junctions along the invasion route, the four corners leading off to Sinderby Heath, Abbots Sinderby, Bag Sinderby and Sinderby le Marsh.

Once there, they pulled on antique ARP armbands, stood boldly in the road and, with encouraging smiles, diverted the Lancashire traffic towards these hamlets. Imagination boggles at what happened in Sinderby le Marsh, because the road fades into one. And, at Bag Sinderby, as its name implies, its only road is its entry and exit and ends in a deep wide dyke. But its approach is four desolate miles long and, car by car, the Mancunians sped joyfully along its deceptive emptiness and filled it. Then, too late for those behind to cry 'Forward!' and those before to cry 'Back!'

Eventually, of course, these pockets filled right back to the main road and the prisoners, working out what had been done to them, cried out for terrible vengeance. But the Twemlowites already had withdrawn in good order to link up with the next diversion ordained to mop up overspill.

For a time, the more intelligent tried to arrange a big

back-out but were undone by the first non-cooperator, who abandoned his locked car and set off walking. I might as well say now as later that, after the match, it was near chaos as would-be escapers tried to burst out through field gates. But as every countryman knows, one field usually only leads into another, and some were trapped until Sunday, when we sent tractors to drag them out. No charge was made for this.

But the real calamity befell the Manchester side itself, who had been in training quarters at Skegness and had put off leaving until after breakfast. (You see, in their heart of hearts, they still didn't take us seriously!) Their coach was trapped in a procession. Three miles to go and the agitation was spreading down from the manager. Two miles away, they stuck utterly at Sinderby Stoupe. Then, after a panic-stricken council, they abandoned the coach and, like earlier pilgrims, took a bearing on our distant steeple and struck off across country. Mind you, they would have done well to have conformed to medieval practice and crossed themselves before venturing into the watery waste – the Stoupe having been placed there for that sensible purpose.

Sinderby & District only stays above water because of these water-courses and every field is bounded by them. And so, the soles of their shoes inches thick with heavy clay, their natty togs soaked and plastered to the knees from misjumps, their tempers in tatters, the weary band ploughed up into the churchyard like souls rising from torment at the Last Trump. They were in such a truly grim condition that Mr Dadds, taking a very broad-minded view of their plight, unlocked the church and let them rest and dry out round his coke stove, which he'd already lit for the next day's Matins.

And there, those furthest from the soothing coke fumes fretted and apportioned blame – a classic seedbed for defeat, even at tiddlywinks.

★

Several football correspondents were lost on the way too. In fact *The Sunday Telegraph* was the only Sunday paper to get through. Their man, Inigo Scobie, had set off the day before 'to smell the wind', as he put it. He had married one of the Board's nieces but wore black boots, and was highly regarded as having the common touch. Actually he excited a lot of interest amongst the villagers, because his very expensive overcoat belied his boots.

I am now quoting the opening lines of his report.

I came to Sinderby Steeple by way of Nun Charnley, Fenny Mauduit and Ewerne Tarrant, a tiny grey-walled settlement, forgotten in the western wolds. In the churchyard where the rude forefathers of the village sleep, great chestnuts reared into the pale winter sky, bare ruin'd choirs where late the sweet birds sang . . .

(I may say that, later, Mr Croser used his report in his Eleven-Plus Class to illustrate atmosphere created by carefully selected words.)

Regrettably, he also got everybody's except Sid Swift's name wrong, but it didn't cause offence because only Alex and Giles took a quality Sunday newspaper, the rest liking their basic news drenched in dressings of bloody murders and the sexual deviations of their betters. Actually, once he got down to the actual game, he was a jolly good writer and I cannot do better than to quote him in full.

STAGGERING THAT'S SINDERBY

In a match of rare excitement Steeple Sinderby Wanderers, the side from the back end of Nowhere, rose at the final fences like a thor-oughbred giving the tiny privileged crowd glimpse upon glimpse of the flush of true greatness. It was performance enough to daunt whichever of the three sides the draw will reveal as their opponents in the Semi-Final of the FA Cup. Nothing in Manchester's experience possibly could have prepared them for the ordeal which they endured, and nothing could have armoured them against the swift and deadly flow of football that engulfed them. At the end of the day, when all was done, they were well content to leave with self-respect. There was nothing for them or, for that matter, any other club, on this parish midden, except dusty defeat.

But there was a time when sheer professionalism came into its own and Manchester dominated the game, but then it was seventy-two minutes too late and Sinderby's determination was not to be cracked. They gritted their teeth and, somehow, held on.

The drive and confidence of the home side's opening assault forced Manchester defenders deeper upon each other. And still the villagers found spaces for Montague, Slangsby and Sledmore to plot, spaces for Wimslow and Montague to run and that single fatal space for the Shooting Star himself to turn and blast the only goal of the match. Yet in the brilliant dawn-of-the-game, Slangsby hit the bar, Montague an upright and, on two occasions, the ball wobbled dangerously along the goal line before Goddard put it clear.

Manchester played to a level of defence no team could have bettered. Assault after assault was repulsed and the two runs by Butlin and a superb flick by Dyson were mere gestures by their own forwards. They could not break out of their own half long enough to sustain a raid to deserve the name of reprisal.

Even so, it was not till the dying quarter that the home side scored, a muddled effort undeserving of the context of so fine a game. From a free kick Slangsby came in fast to have his shot blocked, the sprawling Goddard managing to turn it out to Jennings, who, never having known the great Swift in the days of his glory, dawdled a stride too long. Dispossession and shot were almost one movement. The ball struck the inner angle of upright and crossbar and crashed into a corner of the net.

From that moment Sinderby faced counter-attacks of such

ferocity that, until yesterday, I would have supposed no side could have survived . . .

And yet this Homeric struggle took place in almost Sabbath calm, witnessed by a mere 1,800 privileged people. But, outside the Plow, it is said more than 20,000 fans were sustained by local reporter Alice Trigger's tattered tale of the game . . .

All true: he can't be faulted. And yet it was not all. He saw only the game. And the major drama had moved beyond it, for, as the church clock reminded them that only ten minutes were left and still no equalizing goal, foreboding of disaster spread through orchard and paddock and street black with people. And a strange and awe-inspiring sound rose – a vast meaningless roar that went on and on. Not the usual match noise that surges and sinks, but an animal roar like some primeval creature wounded to the death and questioning its fate. It alarmed me. And not just me, our players began to be jittery. Giles Montagu told me later that he felt that they were being willed to lose, that this great blind multitude would tear them apart in an agony of frustration and destroy, not only them, but the village and, last, themselves.

We were being dragged down by sheer noise.

Then . . . THEN!

Then Mr Fangfoss, in his office of churchwarden, rose to yet more glorious stature. Pondering what he had been told about noise and crowds, he had called out the ringers on standby and put their duty to them. And, at a sign from him, and not a moment too soon, the bells burst into the great Grandsire Triple, which had never been attempted in our belfry since Queen Victoria's Jubilee. It was indeed a Great and Mighty Wonder and such a din quelling all other din can never have been heard before on any football ground, crashing and reeling down upon the village, stunning player and concourse alike.

And, in this truly appalling uproar, the game ended. Though no more than two or three players heard the whistle go. The news just spread as it was seen that some no longer bothered to pursue the ball. Then the bells decelerated and stopped and the crowd stumbled dizzily away in a silence that seemed louder than sound.

But reprisals began. The first victim was Corporal, who, interrupting three skinheads busily knocking out Miss Billison's new cottage windows, was dragged across the green outside the Bull, to be martyred by boots. This was witnessed by an interested audience, until Miss Billison, snatching the nearest weapon, a warming pan, fell upon them from their rear, crying, 'You great louts! Where is your manhood?', dealing pendulum blows amongst watchers and watched without discrimination, hitting one head so hard that the pan lid flew off like a discus, removing three teeth as neatly as surgery from another head's mouth (which had just opened to curse her). The crowd drew back, some to their credit shouting, 'Well done, Missus!', thus encouraging her to drag off by the hair the last attacker sitting astride Corporal and to hammer his head hard on the Preaching Cross – doubtlessly the first time the Faith of his Fathers had any measurable effect upon him.

The two survivors, one clutching his bleeding mouth, then fled into the foldyard at the back of the Bull, where they were cornered by Mr Cory the landlord, who immediately secured the gate.

'There were other'n,' yelled the youth.

'True!' said Mr Cory. 'But you are the only two who've come.'

'The most we can get is probation. We're nobbut first offenders,' one cried. Mr Cory considered this plea and rejected it, declaring it didn't help Corporal's head being their first target, which anyway he disbelieved. He then urged the first offender forward at his big son Edgar, who promptly knocked him down. Whereupon he rose in a rage and, butting furiously forward, collided with the foldyard wall. Edgar would have been prepared to let natural justice take its course had not the youth lashed out with his steel-tipped boots and caught him on the shin. Then execution was brief but terrible and he was dragged before his aghast mate and, though revived with a bucket of water, refused to rise. The second youth was then similarly assaulted whilst the first victim crawled away, his big red hands covering his eyes and weeping.

Meanwhile Mr Fangfoss, finding a clutch of vandals in his circular dovecot smashing the interesting revolving apparatus much praised by industrial archaeologists, slammed the ancient oak door and padlocked it, thus leaving them the same exit as the birds – a narrow funnel in the middle of the stone slab roof.

For the first hour they hammered, banged, kicked and yelled threats, the second hour they throttled down to 'Let us out, Mister, we have the coach to catch,' and by ten at night one was snuffling. Throughout all this, Mr Fangfoss maintained an unremitting silence, only going now and then to put his ear to the door and coming away with what passed as a smile. At dawn, as soon as it began to rain, he let them out.

But the mess, you should have seen the mess. A dozen tombstones upended, at least fifty windows smashed, the church notice board torn down, two lots of railings trampled flat, six young trees broken, the telephone hand-set ripped out and the Swan's two outside benches knocked to pieces . . . I could go on. You'd have thought a tornado had passed that way. And I noticed Dr Kossuth leaning wonderingly over his garden gate, doubtlessly revising yet again his appraisal of the English Condition.

'What do you make of it?' I asked our verger, William Dadds. To which he replied philosophically,

> 'But things like this, you know, must be
> At every famous victory.'

Well, that's one way of looking at it.

As far as the semi-final is concerned . . . but who cares about semi-finals? They provide two teams for the final. No more than that. We were drawn to play Aston Villa, so unlikely a name yet carrying an aura like Buckingham Palace or St Leger, and this same name giving us encouragement, for had not the great Birmingham club, winners of the Cup more times than any other, once been no more than Steeple Sinderby Wanderers? A Sunday-school team managed by a Sunday-school teacher.

There is a report of the game in the Official History, three pages of it. But it can't be any secret now that it was not the actual games that truly interested me. After all, what were they? No more than a ball travelling one way or the other! The fascinating games happened off-stage – our domestic drama. For me the Semi-final wasn't at Wolverhampton amid tempests of cheering. My Semi-final was in the Bull's back-room. Between Sir Edward Furlong and Mr Fangfoss.

Sir Edward Furlong, having capped immense Property coups with a title, had bought Sinderby Parva Hall to match fame and fortune, although prudently spending most of his time in the City keeping a sharp eye on his gold mine. Then, one morning as he was reading his *Daily Telegraph*, he realized that, amazingly, the tide of great events was lapping not in London but around his own doorstep – our village, practically *his* village. It shook him badly. And more so when his secretary told him that, by virtue of the odd guinea here and there, he was President of six local football and cricket clubs and Steeple Sinderby was one of them.

From a lifetime of buying cheap other folks' enterprise and energy and selling it off dear, Sir Edward knew all there is to know about riding winners on someone else's back. One of our committee members, Joe Bleasby, was his chauffeur, and it was Joe who bashfully produced him at our next committee meeting.

'Sir Edward here has come along, because he thinks it fitting to give us all the benefit of his wide experience in Business and Politics as all will appreciate as you might say,' he muttered lamely, looking closely at the floorboards, no doubt willing to join the seafarer beneath them.

Sir Edward, however, did not suffer from this disadvantage of becoming modesty, and bestowing a friendly smile on one and all, took Mr Fangfoss's chair at the head of the table.

'It's the very least I feel I can do,' he said. 'As Bleasby has told you, I've established extremely useful contacts with many influential people and it occurs to me that All This is maybe getting a teeny-bit too big for you good folk. Yes? It is? Quite! Very well, initially, my plan will be to appoint some directors and have my solicitors draw up the necessary papers to enable the club to become a limited company. Now, in this area of football, I have a very, very good City friend on the Arsenal board and already have discussed your difficulties with him and he's given me some sound advice about contingency plans which must be made . . .' So he went on and on, chattering and chattering into a stonier silence. Then, on a fine flourish, he came to a stop, looked amiably around and, clicking down the point of a very expensive pen, re-hashed his oration into an affirmatory proposition.

Some of the committee sought guidance from the smoke-grimed ceiling, some studied Mr Fangfoss, and Joe Bleasby, with native wit having read the signs and portents, but with a wife and four kids to fend for in a tied cottage, put on an outrageously unnatural grin and said 'Yes' (which, as he foresaw, was not taken amiss by either party).

This was a crisis of the first magnitude and it was as well our Chairman, as will be recalled, had been born with his mind made up. 'Gentlemen,' he said pleasantly but very firmly, 'I'm sure all present company would like me to thank Sir Edward here for his words and, if he will retire for a few minutes, they will be considered.' He then leaned back in his chair and joined the ceiling-watchers. But beneath the skin, Sir Edward was still that same Ted Furlong who had elbowed, kneed, heaved and kicked his way to Fame and Fortune.

'No, Fangfoss,' he said, 'I am Club president and it would be improper for me to leave the room. My services will cost our Club nothing. A dozen Wembley tickets, if we get there, to slip to associates as a token of appreciation of their help would fill the bill. And a dozen more for people prominent in local society purely as a public relations exercise.' And he sat back in his chair and smiled reassuringly. It was a very fine smile, the smile of a heart brimming with innocent goodwill and, at Company Annual Meetings, it had silenced many a trouble-maker from daring to question hefty directors' fees on the balance sheet.

All along, I have tried to give the impression that Mr Fangfoss was a remarkable man. Well, he *was* a remarkable man. And, like all the truly great, he knew desperate occasions need desperate remedies. And he also knew the English best understand a firm declaration of intent, boldly, and bluntly put, offering them no shilly-shallying alternative to retreat behind. So, for a moment, he stroked his moustache and fixed our prodigal President with a beady eye. Whilst he, tardily now manning his defences, asked impatiently, 'You have something to say, Fangfoss?'

'Yes, Sir Edward,' our Chairman said. 'First, my title is *Mr* Fangfoss. Second, I speak for all present to ask, "What have you done for us?" Two years ago your secretary sent us a pound, which these days scarcely pays for printing your name on our fixture cards. Since then, we have not seen the hair nor hide of you. But now, here you come along and say you are President and want this and that seen to. Well, you can still be President until the next AGM. For all else you've come too late. At the start of the season we *needed* help, plenty of it, and there'd have been a job for you, and you'd have been made welcome. But not now.

'Now I don't like talking this way to you and, if you'd left the room as you were asked, you'd have come back and been politely told the decision and no reasons to upset you. But you played it rough so you must take it rough. We don't want any second-hand advice from the Arsenal football club. We've got a better team than Arsenal, and we've got better management. And, as for getting a wallet of free tickets for your pals, we all pay for our keep here, and you won't be getting one for yourself unless you pay for it. Well, as you've told us, you're President and, in that capacity, you can sit in for the rest of the meeting, even though you know so little about what we're doing that you must have more time to waste than the rest of us. And now we'll get on with the next business, Mr Gidner . . .'

And he turned from Sir Edward as though he'd dropped through the floorboards.

Sir Edward sat like one stunned, and poor Joe Bleasby didn't know where to put himself. But men like Sir Edward Furlong don't rise to the top for nothing; although their natural decent selves have become embedded deep in money middens, a well-placed kick can still bring them to the surface. He laughed. 'Thank you, Mr Fangfoss,' he said. 'I asked for it and I got it. And deserved it. Good luck and I'll be at Wolverhampton and

Wembley shouting my head off for you. I'll drive myself home, George.' And he got up and went.

And later we went to Wolverhampton and beat the Villa 2–1.

I have now come to a very sad part. It is about Diana.

She hadn't been herself; we'd both noticed that and so had Giles. But we didn't like her left all on her own in a bedroom, so she was lying on the sofa. When it was supper time I went out to the kitchen to do some toast and beans and make the cocoa, and I was there when Alex called out. So I ran back and he had her in his arms like a baby and was talking to her and kissing her, even though he must have known she was gone.

Then he laid her down and stroked her black hair. I hardly expect to be believed but her poor twisted face had altered. Now it was a merry face which he, but not I, had once known. He couldn't speak; he pointed. Then he dropped his head and began to cry.

MINUTES OF A MEETING HELD IN

THE BLACK BULL, MARCH 14TH AT 7.30 P.M.

At the Chairman's request members stood in silence as a token of respect for the late Mrs Slingsby.

Apologies for absence – none.

The Hon Sec read *the Minutes of the Last Meeting* and these were agreed nem. con.

There were no *Matters Arising*.

Mr Slingsby (Capt.), reporting on *Interim Progress*, stated that his team had defeated Hackthorn Young Conservatives (away) 13–0, N. Baddesley Congs Tennis & Football Club (home) 14–0, Bennington British Rail (away) 12–0 and Aston Villa (at Wolverhampton) 2–1. The Chairman commented favourably on these statistics and, at the suggestion of Revd G. Montagu, it was agreed to send a note of congratulation to Miss Dolly Preston, now Mrs Hope-Bowdler, on

J. L. Carr

her wedding. The Vicar pointed out that Mrs Hope-Bowdler had substituted for her husband in a game against us earlier in the season and had performed manfully.

Future activities. Mr Slingsby reported that, resultant on the defeat of Tottenham in the other semi-final, his team's opponents in the Final of the FA Cup would be Glasgow Rangers, a side that had won the Scottish Cup on sixteen occasions, many of these having been successive. He affirmed that this club had a high reputation for sportsmanship, their only lapse being in 1869 when, after drawing with the Vale of Leven in the Final, they had not reappeared for a replay.

The Chairman expressed interest in the reason for this, but Mr Slingsby was unable to shed light on this episode. The Chairman supposed that there must have been a strike on the Caledonian Railway.

Mr Slingsby advised the Committee that this would be the hardest game of the season, listing his reasons as follows –

1. Rangers were assessed by impartial observers as having their best side since the early 1920s, when the great Alexander Morton was in his hey-day.

2. The Scots, in a wider sense, considered this game, the first Final since the merging of the two national competitions, as an affair of National Honour and Prestige, and – more narrowly – as conclusive proof to the English of the superiority of their football sides.

After discussion, it was agreed that playing members should be completely separated from the Mass Media. To this end, *with one dissenting vote*, it was decided that

a. the Hon. Sec. should undertake total responsibility for cooperation with or repulsion of the Media, whichever he thought fit.

b. The Captain and the Vicar should make arrangements for the team to leave the village during the days immediately preceding the game itself, and that their venue should be known to no other person.

After strong protests by the Hon. Sec. that he already was over-powered by normal day-to-day commitments, it was agreed that

(i) there would be no blaming him if he made a mess of things.

(ii) the Chairman should undertake sole liaison with the TV branch of the Media.

The Meeting adjourned at 8.42 p.m.

'Well, I'm pleased we got that fettled up, Mr Gidner,' Mr Fangfoss remarked as the meeting broke up. 'All this blasted publicity argy-bargy . . . my phone's not stopped ringing this last week except when I leave it off the hook. So now we've got it settled who does what, one of my chaps'll unscrew the wires in the morning first thing.'

'Well, that's no problem for me,' I said, 'as I'm not on the phone.'

'You are now,' he said, 'as I've fixed up the Parish Reading Room with two chairs, a table and a bottle of ink and the telephone, a regular office in fact. You'll be able to sit back like a Civil Servant. And if anybody rings me personal or on farm business, particularly the Beet Factory, just jot it down and Mrs Fangfoss'll look in once a day to pick up anything. To give you a start, I've dropped in the post that's come so far . . .'

When we got home, I discussed this with Alex and he said that he was convinced Mr Fangfoss was smiling faintly as he went off. As this was extremely unusual, it gave me a feeling of uneasiness so that I could not sleep, and this was aggravated as the night wore on. In fact, it became so bad that I got up at one in the morning and put a coat over my pyjamas and went up the street to the Reading Room. And it was arranged just as Mr Fangfoss had described it, except for no sign of the letters he had mentioned. But then I noticed four sacks in a cor-ner and, when I examined one, to my astonishment it was full to its neck of unopened letters, and there must have been seven or eight hundred of them, maybe more than a thousand, packed tight in bundles. I mean there was that number in each sack.

I sat down at the table (which was bare except for the ink bottle and steel pen) and started on them. An hour later I found I'd only *read* about thirty, let alone *answered* any, scarcely a skimming off the top of the first sack. And half that thirty weren't even straight-forward letters asking for straight answers. True, there were some easy ones just asking for photographs, which could have been dealt with then and there if we'd had any photographs, and some asking for autographs, which were impossible to get now that we'd agreed about separating the players from everything else. Also, some were from small boys asking how to succeed at football.

But most were either seeking solace or pleading for help in their private problems, nothing to do with football at all. In fact, the more I read the more I realized what pain and anguish there is in this world of ours, and how many folks don't know anyone to go to for healing balm. So they just catch at any name of any human being they hear of on TV or in the papers. There they were, stuck with this great worry over the rent, joyless beds, not getting promotion, being shunned because of bad breath and so forth, and then they happen to hear of a man like Mr Fangfoss or Alex Slingsby or even Sid Swift. Men, unlike them, successful, confident and calm in mind. And they think, Well he seems to have got happiness all sewed up so maybe he can help me out of my mess. So their cries for rescue came pouring in out of the darkness. At this moment literally so.

Dear Mr Fangfoss,

My husband has started going out with a woman he has met at his works' canteen and was definitely seen fondling her . . .

Dear Mr Slingsby,

My boy has left home in a rage with his dad about having the TV turned off and I haven't heard from him for above a fortnight. I think he is running wild in Batley . . .

Dear Mr Swift,

I ordered a set of encyclopoedeas on appro and now they've come I have found that they are beyond me but the encyclopoedea firm won't take them back . . .

In fact, I lost myself in them. Having had this trouble myself, I can well understand the state they had got into and how you don't know where to turn, no one wanting to know about it, even if you could make yourself tell your trouble. It got to be quite cold sitting there while their misfortunes washed over me, but I stuck at it and was making some progress and must have worked my way down at least a tenth of the first sack. Then I heard a car draw up outside and was amazed to find it was light outside and had become morning. So I went to the door to stretch my legs and it was the Post Office van unloading two more sacks of letters. When I saw this, I realized at once that it was hopeless, and humanity would just have to go on suffering until I could organize some First-Aid from another source than myself, and anyway it was discouraging to find none of the letters were to me personally. So I shoved the letters I'd read back into the sack, envelopes and all, leaving the table, except for the ink bottle, bare again. Then, thinking rather disloyally of Mr Fangfoss, I hurried back to snatch an hour on the bed.

From that time on, I gave up any hope of doing anything in the greetings card line or with my research into Thos Dadds, the Peasant Poet. Of course, this was because of the time-factor but only partly. In fact, it was psychological and there came a time when I felt I had lost for good the inclination to write verses. Indeed, it took me several months to be myself again. Like Sid Swift I began to have doubts about life-utilization. Eventually Dr Kossuth straightened me out but, for a while, life was unbearable. (Well, this is not entirely true because I bore it.)

This flood tide of letters came rolling remorselessly in twice a day. Eventually the office table was hemmed in by them and we started to make a second layer. You might suppose that they could have been stored in one of the Chairman's granaries and then winnowed during the summer and winter. But, hidden amongst them were bound to be vital tidings for the football club about something or other. So I mobilized the Old People's Darby & Joan Club to meet daily in the Church, where the pews were ideal for sorting letters, and this they were surprisingly pleased to do because, except for the Pools, most of them received no letters. But this turned out to be not 100% satisfactory, because most of them were slow letter readers or had poor eyesight and, another thing, they got too involved with correspondents crying out for help and began writing laborious letters back, relating their own experiences or the experiences of someone known to them with troubles along the same lines. So I had to take a heartless line and forbid them to take letters home to answer and told them plainly that their only job was to sort out anything that looked remotely like a business letter to do with either Sinderby Wanderers or Mr Fangfoss's farming business. And all the others were to be put back into a bag, and they could answer them to their hearts' content *after* the Cup Final.

But the telephone . . . it never stopped. The queue in the Outside World waiting to make contact with Sinderby must have been hours long and only the persistent persisted. I remember one particularly – he said he was a sheik calling from Muscat in the Gulf of Oman. He kept repeating this as though it was a vital part of his address like a street number – 'Gulf of Oman, Gulf of Oman,' he kept saying. He said he'd seen Biddy's picture in *The Times* and would send the football club all the oil it could use, if we'd order her to be his pen-pal. The price of telephoning didn't seem to bother him at all and he didn't seem to understand that life in Sinderby was much busier for me than things on the lone and level sands were for him. No sooner was the receiver down before it began to ring again. It was quite impossible to get on with any administration, and I couldn't cut the wires because we needed them for outgoing calls.

Eventually I hit on a plan for giving people the idea that they'd had an answer without actually answering them. This was based on the Principle well known in Government and gigantic industrial enterprises that, though a great deal of communication between one department and another is quite mysterious, this must never be admitted.

I have mentioned Corporal. Now, so long as you only gave him one item at a time and allowed not the slightest alternative or diversion, he was quite sensible and useful when it came to cleaning out toilets or mending nets. His drawback was in oral communication, because his memory-filling mechanism was scrambled in the Western Desert, and this took the unusual symptom of answering not *your* question but the last enquirer's, and though the British Legion had paid for him to be looked at by no end of specialists, no one could cure it. So that, if the person on the telephone asked, 'Can we have world rights on The Sid Swift Story?' he got the answer to, 'Will your club sponsor our bedtime drink?' Thus, even the simplest enquiry consumed very satisfactory telephone time as the caller sparred and probed, trying to work out if it was Corporal or himself that was mad. But, oddly, quite a surprising number of people went off the line believing that they *had* been answered, and I put this down to being brainwashed from childhood by commercials, nationalized spokesmen and lying politicians.

Corporal himself was tremendously enthusiastic at his promotion into admin and showed this by fetching his camp-bed down to the Reading Room, eating and sleeping there, although he can't have got much sleep. Later, the Exchange told me that calls kept coming in right through the night from sufferers who had insomnia or who slept when everyone else was up. And there was one woman in mid-Wales who crossed lines by sheer accident and delightedly found that here was one telephone left awake in Britain and a man ready to talk to her and never in a rush to ring off. So, each night, she poured out incoherent instalments of her struggles with her late husband's greedy sisters and with the council surveyor who kept making her pull down extra rooms which she kept having built. And, whilst she was getting her breath back, Corporal told her of little things that had impressed him at the Battle of Alamein, where his last actual contact with the rational world was in winning a Military Medal from it.

Actually, this is fascinating so I shall finish what transpired before moving on . . . this nightly conversation changed this rich Welsh woman's life. Other people she had told her troubles to had always given her good advice or had been scared off by the alarming things that kept happening to her. But Corporal heard her through, and offered no comment, merely continuing his account of his campaign in the desert. In fact, it all is a matter of medical history now and was printed in *New Healing* and, if I might really run on ahead, the woman and Corporal having become almost like the rest of us (though, of course, they were never so happy again), arranged to spend a holiday together at Leamington Spa and later married.

Thus, having sloughed off the correspondence and the

telephone, I was free to face and fend off the pilgrims who had found their way into Sinderby and wanted things. People like the Bishop of Barchester, who made Giles give up his pulpit to him once they started televising the services, and the carpetbaggers who wanted to pour money over us if we would say we used their beer, cigars, deodorants, cars . . . And the most bizarre happening was a string of superb girls from a glossy mag who were photographed modelling new clothes under our goal posts on the Plow and lolling amongst the tombstones. (This latter sequence appeared under the elegaic headline, RUDE FOREFATHERS AND ANIMATED BUSTS.)

Of course, newspaper men came in packs and their published howls brought in Post Office flying squads, so that though for years the Parish Council had petitioned vainly for an extra call-box, this lot, on overtime rates, fitted up half a dozen telephones in the Reading Room whilst I was away resting. But, mindful of the PC's ancient feud, Mr Fangfoss, on the instant, tore them out again – with reporters following him into the street still shouting down dangling wires leading into his pockets. In fact, when this was shown unkindly on TV, the Public thought better of it than *Candid Camera*, and both networks had to repeat it several times so that the GPO was back within the day to erect *two* permanent call-boxes in Back Lane. So, honour satisfied, the landlord of the Swan allowed press phones to be installed in his billiard room at an immense rental. And, from this lair, they roamed our two streets and then the district like ravening beasts listening for any voice willing to join the clamour on their sports page.

Their readers craved for any angle, even the steep angle of a picture of Giles in his pulpit snapped by a camera poked through a squint. This particular feature greatly heartened Rangers supporters, who, unaware of the Bishop's callous substitution, could not visualize this frail old gent slipping past their international backs. The rest of the side stayed well out of reach and only Monkey Tonks, who had to go about his business on the highway, was vulnerable, often being met half-way up garden paths by customers eager to see themselves in next day's paper. The fury of Monkey and the delight of the Milk Marketing Board were in inverse proportion. But, by and large, the sports media was not well served by us and had to rely on the frothing stream pumped out from Glasgow.

Nae doot aboot it, Geordie McGarritty, twenty-eight times capped, is the professionals' professional, one quarter million pounds' worth o' elegant powerrr . . .

That sort of thing, if you care for it.

On the other hand, journalists chasing General News were in clover with Mr Fangfoss at hand to denounce emphatically all aspects of national life. The trade unions, the Common Market, the Irish, the nationalized industries – there had never been such a man for voicing popular prejudice since Enoch Powell retired. And his headlines banged around Britain –

WONDER SIDE'S CHAIRMAN DENOUNCES . . .
THESE THINGS ARE EVIL SAYS FANGFOSS . . .
CHAIRMAN FANGFOSS CALLS FOR . . .

For three weeks it was the nation's diet, and an enterprising young publisher, catching an echo of an earlier best-seller, put out a cheap pocket edition of *Chairman Fangfoss's Words* and sold it in tens of thousands, particularly in the universities.

Meanwhile Mrs Fangfoss, taking the tide at its flood, had circulated a list of grievances to the village people, urging that they should air these when approached by Press or TV, so that, greatly to the annoyance of Authority, the World learnt that our school's toilets were still at the bottom of the playground and froze up in winter, that Sinderby's dustbins were emptied only once a fortnight compared with once a week in Barchester although we paid exactly the same rates, and that the County library wouldn't stock easy-to-read love stories including her own novels.

And, when our Member of Parliament, normally glimpsed only once each five years, turned up with a glad smile for his meed of publicity, aglow with solutions to the world's crises, all he got was nationwide pictures showing him surrounded by dissatisfied consumers of government, demanding why he didn't get off his backside and do something for Steeple Sinderby. Until, having lost his party three opinion poll points, he was hauled back to base. If I hadn't been so personally hard-pressed, I should have found it in my heart to be sorry for him.

But the great and abiding Truth I learnt these weeks was how many people in this world have no Purpose in life, people who live second-hand, sitting all the hours God gives them free of drudgery, staring at either picture papers or TV, waiting like little kids for just another story or for Guidance. And now, before their noses, here was this Real Life Success Story of a Lifetime of people just like them. And these poor souls felt, 'This could happen to me. To *me*! If these humble country folk can do great and memorable deeds, then so can I. Given the chance . . .'

So, what was happening in Steeple Sinderby breathed hope back into hearts withered, rotted and stunted by what life had done to them and what they'd done with life. And each saw our story as it suited him – like the ten blind Indians who described an elephant according to where they took hold of it. So, to some, Mr Fangfoss was all their fathers should have been, a Moses ablaze with prophetic fire, a-brim with wisdom. Alex was a Cromwell, like they too would be from this day forth in the office or on the shop floor, a man of swift, irrevocable decision, unflinching in defence, terrible in execution. And Dr Kossuth was a world-weary think-tank, scorning praise or reward: even Corporal had his adherents.

And a new dimension was added when the *Sun* somehow got hold of a picture of Biddy and cleverly superimposed an exotic gown on her and then did a montage, wide open to unhealthy speculation, of her lounging provocatively with the beautiful Mrs Kossuth in the Swan bar. And, gazing on this vision of delight, from Kirkwall to Penzance, men flinched from what time and carbo-hydrates had done to their once doe-eyed brides and, unmindful of scriptural injunction, 'lusted secretly after strange women . . .'

But if anyone identified himself with me, I never heard of it.

So we were Popular Demand and who can resist Popular Demand? If Popular Demand decrees, then men must smother their grandmas. So be it. And the word went out from reporters camped in the Swan bar that Popular Demand's Top Man was coming. Not the ordinary top man they send to the Cheltenham Gold Cup or the Golf Open but *the* Top Man, Tony Bellman, the Panjandrum before whom trade union moguls and prime ministers fawned or, failing to flatter, cringed. He was superman rightly feared for his devastating ploy of drugging his victims into dazed self-approbation and then blasting them with explosively unanswerable questions. And if the poor wretch, smeared as a fool at best or a rogue at worst, still had enough spirit to falter, 'That's not what I *really* meant . . .' Bellman would thunder, 'Then with respect, WHAT DID YOU MEAN!'

With respect!

His skirmishing outriders began an exploratory assault when I looked in at the Reading Room and found Corporal patiently explaining that Mr Fangfoss was quite satisfied with the fertilizer he presently was using to a woman who was screaming, 'Now look here, YOU! Am I mad or are you mad, my little man! THIS IS TV! TV! Mr Bellman's coming down to do a chat show with one of your locals. YOUR LOCALS! Fongfass or some such! The old parish pump! No, it doesn't matter that you haven't one! And get Lord Pomfret. Mr Bellman's been told Lord Pomfret has a place in the County. Mr Bellman would like him mucking in with the villagers. Mucking in! What do you mean he doesn't use much any more! The rich man in his cottage, the poor man at his gate . . . I'm going crazy! Oh, is he? Then what about his widow? Get her to muck in. What about fertilizer, for God's sake! DON'T YOU UNDER-STAND, YOU OAF, WHOEVER YOU ARE! THIS IS TV!'

As I didn't want to be involved with three new sacks of mail being thrown from a van, I left Corporal answering pleasantly that, if she tried next year after harvest, perhaps Mr Fangfoss would give her a try . . . though he couldn't guarantee it.

I hurried to Howards End and, as best as I could, explained about Bellman to the Chairman, who was the only Briton who'd never heard of him, and hinted that he might do well to feign illness or visit a distant relation. But, since he'd never witnessed one of these nationwide browbeatings, the only impression I made on him must have been my own alarm, because he said kindly, 'Well, as you seem up to the ears in things, Mr Gidner, perhaps I'd better see to him myself.'

And thus it was that our Chairman towered to his peak, and I am told that TV men still speak in awed voice of him. 'We were *used*,' they say. 'An ogre called Fangfoss *used* us. He was Dad of the village and when Dad turned, all did. And Tony Bellman! What he did to that poor bugger! If ever you meet him and he's uppity, murmur "Fangfoss" and watch the sweat drip!'

Of course, by now, our Chairman was a World Figure. For example, I was shown a Tokio front-page, everything in sign-language except MR FUNGFASS, which was the nearest they could render him down. And a newsman told me in awed confidence that *The Times* had originated an obituary file on him. So, on the evening of his TV appearance, Britain's streets were bare, as though there was likely to be a war announced or a Royal Wedding was in progress.

Now the Fangfosses had lived at Howards/Towlers End for many generations. And, as each lot held those that had gone before in veneration, none of their memorials had been shifted from the Front Room, where its current incumbent was now revealed sitting in his great-great-grandfather's Chippendale armchair, waiting to receive the World. And if you are wondering how new memorabilia found a place, it was by hutching everything already there a bit closer, so that if its decor could be said to have had a theme, it must be admitted that this would have to be Cram.

Amongst all this, the camera moved wonderingly about and, all over Britain, fascinated folk cried out in delight, 'Why, look! My dear old grandma had such a thing as that and, when I was a toddler, she let me touch it!' And numerous wives and husbands shrivelled in furious glares because they had discarded onto the council-tip articles now stamped with the Fangfoss seal of domestic desirability. So, from high-rise ghettos where the workers had been herded come the Revolution, to select executive developments (recognizable because they leave the trees standing), force-fed consumers gaped enviously into this bastion against Co-op Instant Furnishing, Scandinavian Functional Design and Sunday Supplement Special Offers.

Here was a dresser hewn by some Tudor Fangfoss from a still writhing oak; there, a 1945 utility armchair, tightly constructed to arrest escape from party political broadcasts, elbowed a gilded spinet inscribed 'York 1745', itself rubbing up against an Indianapolis harmonium, 'Less than the dust beneath thy chariot wheel' propped on its fretwork rest. Above the jump of Spock-trained children, a stout plank circling the room supported coronation mugs, enamelled tea-caddies given away with Rowntree's cocoa and fifty or sixty Staffordshire figures of disastrous generals, evangelical preachers, bruisers and notable felons trembling on eternity's brink.

Festoons of brasses once worn at harvest-home by gone but unforgotten plough-horses, likenesses of Fangfosses, their wooden stares into a bleak future transfixed by journeymen painters, silhouettists and frayed men with almost human tripod cameras; steel engravings of Wm Ewart Gladstone, the infant Wesley being plucked from his father's blazing rectory, the Hundred Deaths of a Drunkard; a framed collection mounted on red plush of regimental cap-badges . . . And, rebuking this watching heathen generation, a truly splendid collection of enigmatic texts, wreathed by pre-Herbicide hedgerow flowers, elaborately stitched by Fangfoss women through black Towlers End winters – WATCH FOR THE NIGHT COMETH, DEEP CALLETH UNTO DEEP AT THE NOISE OF THY WATER-SPOUTS, IT IS BETTER TO MARRY THAN TO BURN . . . and so forth. The stone- slabbed floor was ameliorated with numerous pricked rugs of broadcloth clippings and with fleeces.

The striking gap in this social history of a fenland farming family was a TV set. Our Chairman must have guessed what was passing through the minds of the camera crews because he remarked loudly to the admiring millions, 'We don't have the TV – it gives people ideas – nearly always the wrong 'uns – and, if an idea can't be acted upon, it festers and stinks.'

Tony Bellman did not make his usual bounding entrance (because of the Cram) but he draped himself quite elegantly against the fireplace, only slightly displacing a Tompion clock; 'Now, Arthur Fangfoss,' he said encouragingly, 'tell the Viewing Public how it feels to be Grandpanjandrum of the most talked-of football club in the British Isles.'

'Only men who were lads when I was a lad call me "Arthur",' replied our Chairman. 'The rest call me "Mister". And I don't know what the word you used means. But if it means "Chairman", I feel just like I always do and did. I always feel the same and have done as long as I can remember.'

'Ha, ha,' Bellman said. 'Surely you cannot expect us to believe that, sir.'

Mr Fangfoss's face darkened. 'What is your next question?' he said.

'Our viewers would like to hear your opinion on the Wanderers' chances in the Final.'

'Who can tell? Only a poor booby would say who'll win any game, even holey-holey.'

'Holey-holey?'

'It's marbles. Lads play it. And only Mr Gidner, our honorary secretary, is authorized to make public statements about football. I can answer no more questions about football.'

'But it's what this interview is about. The nation wants your views about football.'

Mr Fangfoss did not answer, staring fixedly at the camera and through it at the Viewing Public, which mostly nodded sycophant-like back at him. And, in the howling silence, the camera settled maliciously on Bellman, who was sweating slightly. But he rallied.

'You have no wages to pay, sir. Yet your committee must have amassed several thousands of pounds. My public would like to hear how you mean to dispose of this.'

'Not their business. Our business.'

'But this is a matter of Public Concern. Even *you* must

acknowledge *that*,' exclaimed Bellman, a note of savagery tingeing his tone.

'Matter of *Private* Concern,' our Chairman replied evenly. 'And Englishmen have not so long noses as such as you make them out to have. Most Englishmen are sick to death of politicians and jacks-in-office and know-alls telling us who we are and what we want. The English are just what they always were – quiet, decent folk saddled with parasites . . .'

'Parasites?' Bellman managed to get in.

'Them that make folk buy what they don't want, them that unnaturally prolong their education, them that make their living asking questions they don't want to know the answers to . . . I could go on for twenty of your programmes. They're like fleas but that they settle in swarms. And they're multiplying. Take that whining twenty-year-old they put on probation in yesterday's paper, the one who starved his three kids while he spent the Public Assistance on booze and fags. We English want him working or starving. If he won't stick to a job, the Public Assistance should chain him to one. Aren't there no salt mines in Cheshire? And, to stop him fathering more of his own breed, castrate him . . .'

The Producer cut it quickly and substituted PLEASE DON'T ADJUST YOUR SET. THIS IS A TEMPORARY DISORDER. Too late, of course.

FORCED LABOUR FOR WORK-SHY* *Mirror*
BRITISH RULING CLASS CALLS FOR CASTRATION
OF RECIDIVISTS* *Pravda*

'My God! I expect you even believe in hanging then?' Bellman exclaimed.

'Certainly! Some English and any number of Irish, Scots and Welsh need hanging as a warning to the rest.'

'Well, we'd better change the subject. Sex now! My research-ers tell me that you have an advanced stand on Sex.'

'Sex!' exclaimed our Chairman, scandalized.

'Yes,' hissed Bellman, throwing his all into a last despairing attack. 'I am told you follow Old Testament Writ and have sev-eral wives.'

Mr Fangfoss did not immediately reply. The suspense was terrific: many people swore they found it more thrilling than the Cup Final.

Then, with immense deliberation, he said, 'Look, you cheeky young louse, before you creep back under your stone, listen here! You do, yes you really do believe folks so yearn to be shown on TV that they'll strip down to the last clout. Well, I'm not some show-biz baboon or politician who will grin through your slimy gibes just so you let him push his grapefruit face into people's hearths and home . . .' And he unexpectedly bent forward so that his face went out of focus and one immense eye menaced the nation. 'And now I want to be switched off, because if you're TV, then thank God I don't have to harbour you in *my* house. But I'll have my full fee, and you'd best pay it or I'll sue you, and I'm a rich man who can afford justice.'

Then, with rarest genius, the camera settled on the text, WHAT CAME YE INTO THE WILDERNESS TO SEE? A REED SHAKEN BY THE WIND? And back to Bellman's face. And faded.

Naturally, this was the most astonishing TV interview of all time and the daily delivery of mail rose to eleven sacks. I could do no more than dip into them, but the few I hurriedly read showed that the Viewing Public (except for a few Scots, Welsh and Irish) was solidly behind our Chairman.

Of the sample I looked at, four contained offers to purchase items seen in his front room, three suggested targets for fur-ther hammer-blows at Authority, one begged him to be godfather to his son, Arthur, at a baptism in Todmorden, one was an offer of marriage ('or anything else as I'm not the fussy sort') and two pleaded with him to stand for Prime Minister.

And so those astonishing last weeks rolled on their way, their hysteria and passion penetrating even Parliament. I quote *Hansard* –

Speaking on the Adjournment, the Hon. Member for Salford said that he spoke for many when he said that he was sick of the Hon. Member for Upper Clydeside's whining and griping (loud protests from Both Sides of the House) and did the Hon. Member suppose that his own hard-working Lancashire constituents had been ordained by God-Almighty to featherbed the Scots? (Uproar) His constituents in past ages had suffered much from their thieving raids and they had had enough. If Scots members of all Parties expected to be taken seriously that their countrymen were God's gift to the Human Race, would they care to explain why, year after year, their fellow aborigines had trooped in their smug thousands to see Celtic play Rangers for their Knock-Out Cup and Rangers play Celtic for their League Championship? These tedious rituals confirmed his Lancashire constituents' fixed opinions that far from being a Lion Rampant, a more suitable insignia would be a toothless beast scarcely able to clean up its incontinence with its own lick-spittle. (At this point the Hon. Member for Salford was called to order by the Speaker but shouted his refusal to apologize for what was the truth.) All right (the Hon. Member shouted), soon, for the first time, some of their tin gods would be venturing south of the Border (but not passing through Lancashire he hoped) where a mere village side was con-sidered match enough for them . . . (At this point the Hon. Member was dragged from his place and struck several times . . .)

This was joyfully bannered by the Press and things began to burn and blaze merrily. ITV sent a cameraman with five coach gangs from Glasgow to cover shop windows methodically being shattered the length of Newcastle-on-Tyne's main street, their proprietors kicked to the ground and Scotsmen having their heads screwed off by policemen. Within an hour of this being shown on TV, the Edinburgh–King's Cross express was halted in Durham station while its entire load was dragged out and forced to cross to the Up-Platform and board a train back north.

I could go on about this. Violence reached such a stage that it was thought that the Final itself either would be cancelled or played in France or Ireland.

And, amidst this uproar, the game galloped towards us. But on the last Tuesday, the team and two reserves boarded a bus at five in the morning and, with Mr Winship himself at the wheel, slipped away, only Alex and Giles knowing its destination. When, by mid-day, it dawned first on the reporters in Sinderby and then worldwide that they'd gone, it was as if they'd slipped off the end of the earth. Immediately a massive search was set afoot.

VILLAGE FINALISTS DISAPPEAR
WHERE ARE THE WANDERERS?

And their pictures were published like Police Wanted bills.

HAVE YOU SEEN THESE MEN?

Actually, they went to Tarrington Upwey Vicarage, which is remote and alone – a good mile even from its own church and up a dead-end track, near the Lincolnshire coast. There the Vicar, a college friend of Giles, put them up in his many bedrooms and attics and his wife fed them good plain food. And, twice a day, they trotted up and down the sands, fortified by cold North Sea breezes and wonderingly discussing what had befallen them on the long road to Wembley from the sandhills of Snainton-on-Sea. In-between time they slept. Only the Rangers had Cup Final nerves. TV and the papers said so. So they *had* to have them.

On the Friday afternoon, the Wanderers were moved south to a discreet private hotel in Enfield and, on Saturday, they quietly made their way to the stadium through the madding, unrecognizing crowds.

And, equally unrecognized, were the Doctor and Mrs Kossuth as they arrived in London to visit an exhibition of Tudor worthies at the National Portrait Gallery. ('Those faces, Mr Gidner, those cool, shrewd faces concealing such fire . . . ah, what a nation we were!')

For me, there had been so much to do that I surfaced at Wembley in a daze, and only recalled that this was the end we'd been struggling towards these many months when the boring worn-out preliminaries were almost over and they had reached 'Abide with Me', that vast, turgid, hopeless roaring of men swilling pity over themselves because their poor old mum was dead, their wife no longer the bright-eyed girl she'd been, their hopes of winning the treble-chance unfulfilled . . .

Then great and mighty roars as the two sides ran out, all heads pecking like hens at programmes, identifying these unknown players from the back of beyond. This became an easier exercise when they were rounded up and formed into lines to be displayed to Royalty, which, fired by a like curiosity, had come in embarrassing force to squeeze minor football officials from the best seats. Alex later told me with mild satisfaction that they shook hands with the Sinderby side as if, for once, they really wanted to meet the owners of the hands. And, installed in the Royal Box, they then were seen to examine with great interest and amiability our Chairman and his two wives.

I think it was only at that moment that I really understood the significance of it all, I mean all that I've given account of. Ginchy Trigger nudged me. 'D'you think we'll win, Joe?' she said. Win? Frankly I'd never thought about it. Nor talked about it to Alex. For the house had been a very quiet place with Diana gone. We didn't talk football any more now. Just looking at him, nothing showed and people supposed that he'd taken it in his stride, perhaps even welcoming freedom from a burden. But I knew different. He'd lost a piece of his life and he would never forget her; she would always be the bright, merry girl on a bike. And, when he thought he was alone, I'd heard him singing quietly

> 'She stepped away from me, and she moved through
>   the fair,
> And fondly I watched her move here and move there.
> And then she went homeward, with one star awake –
> As the swan in the evening moves over the lake . . .'

And I knew that only on the field of play, in the ebb and flow of action, wrapped in a cold determination, could he forget. And that's how the Scots would find him. Not playing for fame or cash or even for Sinderby Wanderers. Just to forget.

'Will they *win*, Joe?' she shouted irritably.

And thinking of all this, 'Yes,' I shouted back. 'Yes, he'll win.' Then they were at it.

I suppose it must have been the most described game of football ever played. I don't mean described just in the Sunday and Monday papers but in the months and years that followed: there isn't a football anthology that doesn't play that game again. If Rangers had done this or Sinderby had done that, if McGarritty hadn't ballsed up that opening, if Monkey Tonks had behaved like a normal human keeper and had gone off for treatment when his hand was trodden on, if, if, if, if . . .

As is well known, it was o–o at full time and the referee later said that he'd allowed no more than a couple of minutes extra to make up for time lost clearing the pitch of exultant Scots when they thought that Kelso had scored in the 89th minute. My own favourite purple patch covering it was by Nigel Kelmscott-Jones in *The Times*. He wrote so well you never would have guessed that both his prep and public schools played rugger, or that he loathed all games and was just filling in with sport until his uncle could find an excuse to winkle out their Paris correspondent . . .

And so the allotted span ended but for these three minutes when the field was black with Scots celebrating Kelso's offside goal: it seemed that this Homeric struggle must now drag itself into an anti-climax of extra-time. But here we still were, drowning in the surge and thunder . . . and two of the minutes were gone and we were shaken into a final convulsion as the conflict rose to a new pitch of fever.

No one there can ever forget it. The ball went mad in the Sinderby area. McGarritty, racing in, cannon-balled it, felling McIver to a writhing heap. And now Airey blasted it to bound from the bar to Kelso on the wing. He slipped past Hardcastle, Ormskirk and Crum-mack, wheeled and lifted the ball in a lazy curve back into the maelstrom.

Tonks rose at it only to be carried despairingly away by a Sinderby man, perhaps Maidstone, leaving McGarritty clear to head it in. But Wimslow rose through the turf – for from where else could he have come? – and turned it out again, and the still agonized McIver, crawling towards it, brought down Airey with the goal open before him . . . Airey – Kelso – McLeod – Airey – Sterling – McGarritty – Kelso – Airey . . . Sinderby are on the rack and now at last surely they must break. Back they come again, a red rampaging wave overwhelming the English side . . . they *must* score. And then . . . and then . . .

And then the truly magnificent Slingsby, who had withstood this assault like a rock, gathered the ball and, on the turn, squeezed a fierce low kick from the scrum. And one wondered . . . one wondered if this had been plotted months ago when this village side was still lost in the obscurity of the midland plains. It had been All or Nothing. Nothing if McGarritty had scored, Nothing if Wimslow hadn't risen from the earth . . . if, if, if . . .

And then . . . I had forgotten him, the Rangers, lured into this trap, had forgotten him, all Wembley had forgotten him . . . and then the immortal Swift, lurking near the centre-spot, took the ball and, without a check in pace, burst into the Scottish half like a rocket, a stream of yellow and red spurting behind him, and in such an awe-ful stillness as Wembley can never have known, even on a midwinter midnight.

The wretched McClusky advanced from his goal, retreated, advanced again and when the majestic shot came, leapt hopelessly in the wrong direction. It struck the crossbar like a thunderclap. Then, as it bounded back, Wembley exploded. Those that sat stood, those that stood leapt, McClusky scrambles back to his line, Slingsby comes in at great speed, takes the ball on his chest, controls, steadies and hammers it into the pit of the goalman's stomach. And he, wrapped up like a parcel, collapses into the back of the net, guiltily trying to detach the ball from his person.

It was a finale molto larghetto ff in C Major (of course) to this feat unparalleled in the history of British sport.

Well, he was right, because that Final Game *was* like a piece of great music and, some might say, complete in itself. But, looking back as only three or four of us could, this tremendous climax of crashing double chords was no more than a fragment of a greater whole.

I often wish that I could have known the end at the beginning, so that each detail could have been savoured as it happened. But then, life isn't a gramophone record one can play again and again till one feels one understands it. It is Now or Never for most of us, and we haven't the time. But we shall tomorrow . . .

There was some official junketing which had to be endured and, no doubt, some of our lads enjoyed it and Alex recognized this. Then they sat round the changing room, exhausted yet exhilarated, and he knew something was expected from him.

'Well, chaps,' he said, 'that's it – the finish. For me, anyway. You as well, Sid?' And Sid nodded. 'Things'll sort themselves out in a couple of weeks. Give us at least that. I'm sure the Committee will see you all have a really big hand-out when we divvy up. I expect it will be in proportion to the cup-ties you've played in and some of the normal league games will count as well. You'll understand that the minute you take the money it makes you professionals and, if you have offers from other clubs, the full transfer fee will be yours. But you must give us a couple of weeks to sort things out, eh, Joe?'

I nodded and, to tell the truth, I couldn't speak.

'And Joe,' he went on, 'thanks – you've done a miracle of a job.' And they all turned towards me and began clapping. It was a proud moment.

'It's the end of the Wanderers as we know them. Next year, it will be back to the villages' league. Perhaps it would be better to start under a new name – "United", "Athletic", something like that. But that's for the new Committee to decide. But we've done what we set out to do and this is the end of the road. That mayn't make much sense to some here. You'd like it all again. But listen, it wouldn't be like that: a second helping has never the same savour. So we'll call it quits and be saved from the ancient ill of dust-in-the-mouth. And the withered laurels (if I'm to be allowed a bit of airy-fairy, Joe?). Well, why not? All teachers have the right to dish out an extra ration of extra-mural preaching. Let's brood on Fame & Glory. And clinging on too long . . .'

Then he paused; quite unexpectedly he grinned. 'Well, we're finishing on a fanfare. No "that strain again: it hath a dying fall" for you. Now you will not swell the rout of lads that wore their honour out, runners whom renown outran and the name died before the man . . .' He raised an eyebrow quizzically at me, and I'd like to think he meant, Well, at least *you* know what I'm on about.

Some looked blank, Sid gazed at his boots, Giles looked as though he took it in and the rest looked as though they were trying to.

'That's all. You're off the hook now.' He laughed. 'Off *my* hook, anyhow.'

And we all began to laugh too, some a bit hysterically.

And then . . .

And then we went home. Mr Fangfoss to his plains of sugar beet, Mrs Fangfoss to Howards End and diminishing literary fame, poor Beattie to stir passion's dying embers in barn and byre, Alex to his empty home, Giles to laborious sermons, Ginchy to inquests, funerals and council meetings, me to pick away at my monograph on Thos Dadds the Verger Poet. Biddy and Sid to their teach-ins and demos. And I envied the Kossuths, who had not 'come up' and so hadn't to climb down again.

On fine weekends, tourists drove slowly round Front Street and Back Lane or parked and strolled around gaping, then going away cross at finding it was just another dull village, where no one had looked particularly pleased to see them or could be drawn out about what had happened. The goalposts had been taken from Parson's Plow, and you would have needed science fiction imagination to have seen an orchard black with silent people gazing up into the barren trees or to have heard the baying crowds overpowered by bells or Mr Greenslade's double-barrelled hymn of joy. Steeple Sinderby was another empty theatre, the dust was gathering, the actors gone away.

When the papers reported that the Club was disbanding, every player had some sort of offer from league sides and Sid, Alex and Monkey Tonks had a dozen. But only five signed forms and took transfer money. Monkey was one who didn't: he married Maisie Twemlow and made it clear that further cavortings wouldn't do their milk-round any good at all, and that she must damp down her demonic fire by keeping the books and setting out at five in the morning on the round now and then. And he never played football again. Never. And, if you looked at him from that time forth, all you saw was a milk-man with numerous long knitted yellow scarves.

The share-out came to as much as £5,000 for some players and even reserves in village games got as much as £150. £2,000 was voted into a Trust Fund for Corporal, interest to be paid out strictly weekly and, when he died, the capital to revert to the Grimsdyke Bread Dole. Another thousand pounds went towards the Church Bells Fund, and there was the thousand I mentioned at the beginning, five hundred down and five hundred when I've written the Official History.

And things settled back into their old tracks and it was grand to be back trundling monotonously along them again.

And then . . .

And then it didn't work out like that. These things had happened and now nothing would – could be ever the same again. Well, could it?

The part Dr Kossuth had played had not been lost on the Hungarians. Things took a turn for the better there, and they stopped knocking down doors at three in the morning. Our triumph was trumpeted as a triumph for the nation of Ferenc Puskás, and the Kossuths were brought back from exile like royalty. 'Not me,' the Doctor told us as he left. 'England has my heart and an Englishman I'll die. Sinderby is enough for me, Mr Fangfoss. It is my dear wife; *her* heart, alas, is in Hungary and I love her deeply. There is nothing for it but to return there.' And they did. He was made Chancellor of his old university and, when they had a baby, it was very touching because they named it Alexander Sinderby Kossuth. A man called Perkins took his place as head of the school, and he was a nice man and did his best. Mrs Perkins, poor woman, was no Mrs Kossuth; no pulses quickened as *she* trotted to the sub-post office. But she had a heart of gold, poor soul!

And Alex left too. There was a job advertised for a one-teacher school, with croft attached, on a tiny island in the Inner Hebrides, and they appointed him without an interview as no one else applied for it. Though he'd have got it anyway, because he was as reluctantly admired up there as was the formidable Larwood when he moved to Australia.

'No,' he explained to me. 'I'm not going to stay there for ever, so there's no sense in selling the house the way inflation is. You can have it to rent cheap till I feel like coming back in four or five years' time. It'll give me time to think things straight again. Some things I want to remember and some to forget. *You* don't need to be told, Joe.'

And off he went with, seemingly, no regrets. I heard later that his island got full tourist treatment from the McBain Shipping Line on trips from Oban. Mercifully, there was no harbour but, on day tours to Iona and Fingal's Cave, they used to lay offshore for five or six minutes to let Rangers supporters have long brooding looks through binoculars at his school and cottage. And, it is said that only one or two muttered that the island's name should be altered to St Helena.

As for Sid, I can't do better than quote *The Times*. And not the Sports Pages either.

Mr Sidney Swift, the association footballer, who was largely instrumental in a remote village's extraordinary feat of winning a premier sporting trophy, is to visit the Chinese People's Republic where he will advise on the preparation of their World Cup teams.

Mr Swift stated that he had stipulated that Miss Belinda Montagu must accompany him and that there should be no restriction on her missionary work in the furtherance of her Religion. The Chinese Government also had agreed that there should be no restriction on his distribution of free copies of *Mr Fangfoss's Words*. Mr Swift also added that nothing could induce him to play football again or to accept remuneration for his advice. From now on, he stated that his intention was to devote his life to worthwhile pursuits.

And me . . . and my love affair, temporarily in abeyance, with Ginchy Trigger. Well, I finally made up my mind that we could make a go of it and perhaps someday, age would adjust her into a home-body. After what happened that night on Parson's Plow, I could foresee that living with her would have its pleasures as well as pain. All the same, I went for a long tramp over Howards End way to make certain that it really was what I wanted. There would be no altering her, I finally decided. She always would prefer men's company to women's, slacks to skirts, the Snug to the Saloon, bash-bash to classical and Mess to Order. But it would be nice to be sure one familiar face stayed around.

I found her in her shed with a carburettor in bits and an oil smear on her nose, which gave her a wonderfully engaging

look. She heard my proposal with great interest, as usual looking too believing and, when I'd finished, said, 'Well, I feel
honoured, Joe. I feel very honoured because I can see from
your shoes that you've not come to this decision lightly. And, in
the ordinary way of things, I might have said Yes.' (Then she
kindly changed this to, 'I would have said Yes.')

'But I'm spoken for, as they say. Giles asked me last week. He
hasn't bought me a ring, as they haven't handed over the Easter
Offering yet. But the big day's in June. Mr Fangfoss is going to
give me away and then we're going to have a big Wedding Supper in one of his barns, like *Far from the Madding Crowd*, and
you're going to be asked to propose the chief toast to the bride.'

'But you'll never make a parson's wife, Ginchy dear,' I burst
out. 'You . . .'

'Oh yes I will,' she answered very firmly, remembering the
night of the Leeds game we spent on Parson's Plow and guessing my meaning. 'And, anyway, we shan't stay here. He's got a
chaplain's job at Foxberrow College in West Africa, at a place
called Sinji where he's heard they're keen on cricket and the
sun never stops shining. And the Principal, a Mr Harpole, has
promised me a job teaching mechanical engineering.'

'But what about your ambitions?' I said '*The Sunday Times*
and a TV Spot.'

'No,' she replied. 'What I want is a house of my own, with a
husband in it and, after a while, two boys and two girls. Then I
think I might start a WI out there. And so on . . .'

And so we parted, and I went for another walk, this time
beyond Howards End, and it was true what Mr Fangfoss had
said – there *were* only more sugar-beet fields. On my way back,
I met Mrs Kossuth and hinted at all this to her.

'Well, Mr Gidner,' she said, turning her blinding smile on
me, 'one man can't know what another man sees in a woman,
now can he? Maybe dear old Giles needs the sort of woman

who *does roar* around – to turn him on, as you say. For instance, how could *you* know why my Johannitsa needs *me*? But I mustn't make dolly-chat or you will be thinking I am not a true-blue Britisher . . .' And she went off into beautiful peals of laughter.

Dr Kossuth is a very lucky man and I didn't know his name was Johannitsa.

So, at the end, our Chairman, Mr Fangfoss, was the only one of the big ones left behind. Naturally, as you'd expect, he took all that had happened as something that had happened. 'Che sera, sera,' he told me. (His son was learning that language now.) 'I'm returning my full energies to my other offices, which have been somewhat neglected these last few months, also to my husbandry.'

So his first project was to convert the defunct Primitive Methodist Chapel into a Cup Final memoral Museum and laid down that all profit must be used to get the building back into use for Divine Worship. Madame Tussauds made him wax fig-ures of all the players and also one of himself and, by inserting 10p, a machine recited all the scores of that season's games and then reproduced our church bells quelling the roaring crowd. It's well worth a visit when in the district, though don't expect another Woburn. But you will see Miss Billison – she's the curator.

But it seemed that all that had happened meant no more to him than a good harvest. This perplexed me thoroughly. Could anyone *really* take these things in his stride? 'Che sera, sera' and forget? Well, seemingly our Chairman could. But he was a very remarkable man.

If only I could have shut the door like him. Sometimes on a Saturday, when I feel I need a change from writing verses or the Official History or my Thos Dadds monograph, I walk down Front Street about tea-time, when the village is behind curtains checking the Pools against TV. And then it all comes back.

And it hurts. Times I could vomit remembering. I have to stop and lean on a wall or something. Fancy! this street – once a great flood of fans! And the orchard of fruitless trees – black with a mob stunned into silence! And Parson's Plow, our forwards flickering up and across it – silent now as in a dream! Alex, Sid and all the lads!

And it is so sad to know that those days, win or lose, can't return. Nor those remembered faces be gathered into one place again.

I was stood there by the Preaching Cross in the dusk one Saturday in January and, the next thing I knew, Mr Fangfoss was there as well. 'Mr Gidner,' he said, 'I know what you're looking for. But it's gone, and it'll never come back.'

Then – and only for an instant – our Chairman gave himself away. 'And more's the pity, lad,' he said.

Botley, 1974.

PENGUIN MODERN CLASSICS

CIDER WITH ROSIE
LAURIE LEE

'I had ridden wrapped up in a Union Jack to protect me from the sun, and when I rolled out of it, and stood piping loud among the buzzing jungle of that summer bank, I feel, I was born.'

Cider with Rosie, Laurie Lee's bestselling autobiography, immortalized an era and a place. In it he recalls the glories of a country boyhood in the beautiful Slad valley in Gloucestershire. His was a slow, mellow England, one 'of silence ... of white roads, rutted by hooves and cartwheels, innocent of oil and petrol'. It is an unforgettable elegy to a world that has all but vanished.

'It distils and preserves the essence of a bygone rural age and the heady spirit of childhood which haunted it' *The Times*

With an Introduction by Susan Hill

read more ⓟ

PENGUIN MODERN CLASSICS

UNDER MILK WOOD
DYLAN THOMAS

'[Its] great strength is the Chaucerian life and liveliness of its sixty or more characters, enjoyed in all their spontaneous eccentricity' Walford Davies

As the inhabitants of Llareggub lie sleeping, their dreams and fantasies deliciously unfold. There is Captain Cat surrounded by fish that 'nibble him down to his wishbone', Mog Edwards, 'a draper mad with love' for shy dressmaker Miss Price, Organ Morgan, listening to the music in Coronation Street with 'spouses ... honking like geese and the babies singing opera', while at the sea-end of town, Mr and Mrs Floyd lie in their bed 'side by side ... like two old kippers in a box'. Waking up, their dreams turn to bustling activity as a new day begins.

In this classic modern pastoral, the 'dismays and rainbows' of the imagined seaside town become, within the cycle of one day, 'a greenleaved sermon on the innocence of men'.

Edited with an Introduction and Notes by Walford Davies

read more   (penguin logo)

PENGUIN MODERN CLASSICS

LARK RISE TO CANDLEFORD
FLORA THOMPSON

LARK RISE/ OVER TO CANDLEFORD/ CANDLEFORD GREEN

'Our literature has had no finer remembrance in this century, no observer so
genuinely enduring' John Fowles, *New Statesman*

The story of the three closely related Oxfordshire communities – a hamlet, the
nearby village and a small market town – this immortal trilogy is based on Flora
Thompson's experiences during childhood and youth. It chronicles May Day
celebrations and forgotten children's games, the daily lives of farmworkers and
craftsmen, friends and relations – all painted with the gaiety and freshness of
observation that make this a precious and endearing portrayal of country life at the
end of the last century.

With an Introduction by H. J. Massingham

PENGUIN MODERN CLASSICS

HANGOVER SQUARE
PATRICK HAMILTON

London 1939, and in the grimy publands of Earls Court, George Harvey Bone is pursuing a helpless infatuation. Netta is cool, contemptuous and hopelessly desirable to George. George is adrift in a drunken hell, except in his 'dead' moments, when something goes click in his head and he realizes, without doubt, that he must kill her ...

In the darkly comic *Hangover Square* Patrick Hamilton brilliantly evokes a seedy, fog-bound world of saloon bars, lodging houses and boozing philosophers, immortalizing the slang and conversational tone of a whole generation and capturing the premonitions of doom that pervaded London life in the months before the War.

'One of the great books of the twentieth century' *Independent on Sunday*

'A masterly novel ... you can almost smell the gin' Keith Waterhouse, *Spectator*

PENGUIN MODERN CLASSICS

THE HAUNTING OF HILL HOUSE
SHIRLEY JACKSON

Alone in the world, Eleanor is delighted to take up Dr Montague's invitation to spend a summer in the mysterious Hill House. Joining them are Theodora, an artistic 'sensitive', and Luke, heir to the house. But what begins as a light-hearted experiment is swiftly proven to be a trip into their darkest nightmares, and an investigation that one of their number may not survive.

The best-known of Shirley Jackson's novels and filmed twice as *The Haunting*, this is an immaculate examination of how fear can make us our own worst enemy.

'Stepping into Hill House is like stepping into the mind of a madman; it isn't long before you weird yourself out' Stephen King

PENGUIN MODERN CLASSICS

WE HAVE ALWAYS LIVED IN THE CASTLE
SHIRLEY JACKSON

With an Afterword by Joyce Carol Oates

'A marvellous elucidation of life ... a story full of craft and full of mystery'
The New York Times Book Review

Living in the Blackwood family home with only her sister Constance and her
Uncle Julian for company, Merricat just wants to preserve their delicate way of
life. But ever since Constance was acquitted of murdering the rest of the family,
the world isn't leaving the Blackwoods alone. And when Cousin Charles arrives,
armed with overtures of friendship and a desperate need to get into the safe,
Merricat must do everything in her power to protect the remaining family.

In her final novel, Shirley Jackson displays a mastery of suspense, family
relationships and black comedy.

PENGUIN MODERN CLASSICS

THE TITMUSS NOVELS BY JOHN MORTIMER

PARADISE POSTPONED

'Ironic and elegant ... a panoramic human comedy of life in our times' *Evening Standard*

When Simeon Simcox leaves his entire fortune to the ruthless, social-climbing Tory MP Leslie Titmuss, the Rector's two sons react in very different ways. Henry decides to fight the will and prove their father was insane. Younger brother Fred takes a different approach, digging in Simeon's past, only to uncover an entirely unexpected explanation for the legacy.

A delicious portrait of English country life by a master satirist.

TITMUSS REGAINED

'Richly entertaining ... mercilessly funny in its observations on the way we live now' *Sunday Times*

The Right Honourable Leslie Titmuss has clawed his way up the Tory ranks and is now Secretary of State at the Ministry of Housing, Ecological Affairs and Planning. But seismic changes are afoot in the countryside where a new town threatens to engulf his back garden. Will Leslie bow to market forces? Or will he fight against the multi-storey car parks and shopping precincts that could sweep away Rapstone Valley?

The sequel to *Paradise Postponed*, *Titmuss Regained* is an affectionate elegy to a disappearing world.

THE SOUND OF TRUMPETS

'Delicious ... Mortimer in vintage form' *Observer*

When a Tory MP is found dead in a swimming-pool wearing a leopardskin bikini, the embittered Titmuss sees the ideal opportunity to re-enter the political arena. All he needs is a puppet, and Terry Flitton – inoffensive New Labourite – is perfect. Terry heads blindly for the by-election but is he too busy listening for the sound of victory trumpets to notice that the Tory dinosaur is not quite extinct?

The culmination of a masterly trilogy, *The Sound of Trumpets* is a devilishly witty satire on political ambition, spin and sleaze.